Where A Demon Hides

War of the Second Iteration - Coda

by

Thomas Watson

Where a Demon Hides: War of the Second Iteration – Coda

by Thomas Watson

Cover Artwork by Fiona Jayde Media

ISBN: 9798364757463

DEDICATION

For the fans of War of the Second Iteration, who just couldn't leave well enough alone. And thank goodness!

ACKNOWLEDGEMENTS

Thanks to Steven Howser, Stephanie Carrell Hansen, and Linda Watson for their willingness to wade through the earlier drafts of this story. You made a difference, and not small one.

CONTENTS

A Note from the Author

Where a Demon Hides was written as a coda to the five-part *War of the Second Iteration*. The story takes place two years after the events of the fifth and final volume of that series, *Setha'im Prosh*. Readers have asked, since then, about what they see as a loose end regarding one of the main characters. Although I did not think of it as a loose end at the time, once the question was asked of me, and I considered it, a story began to grow. Hence the telling of this tale.

A few Leyra'an phrases you might find useful:

Eli'sana: literally sister-wife, a phrase describing a female member of a blended household.

Ara'sana: literally brother-husband, the male equivalent of eli'sana.

Isi'sani: "my child from another;" applied, by one who is not the biological parent, to a child born to a blended household.

1. Awareness

Alicia awoke to nothing.

There was only the awareness of self, beyond which – *nothing*. She was frightened and confused. Lost. There were no boundaries; nothing contained her. She was open and vulnerable with no way to hide. For some reason, she very much wanted to conceal herself, but her *self* was all there was. There was nowhere to go.

Memories flickered at the edge of her fear, just within reach, and she clutched at them. They were horrible, the stuff of nightmares, but they were better than nothing — almost. Mind-shattering pain and a blinding light behind her eyes. She felt screaming rage mingled with tearing grief. And then she was dead. She was sure of this, so sure of her personal extinction that awareness was a painful shock. She existed and remembered, but the memories were brief and then, once again, there was – nothing.

Death.

This?

Terror surged through her and threatened to become madness, a ripped and ragged edge to her raw sense of self. But before it could fully grip her there was a voice. A familiar voice, in her and around her, much beloved. Hope swelled within the terrible, formless nothingness of it all. Alicia yearned toward that voice.

"Alicia, wake up," it said. "Please, it's time. Wake up. Come back to me."

She heard, but she could not respond. Alicia wanted so very much to answer that voice. And yet with hearing alone came a sudden sense of true existence, a jumbled awareness of her own physical form; it all felt disconnected. She was exhausted. Bone-deep weariness filled the disparate bits of her. There was relief at feeling such things, feeling anything at all; relief so intense it verged on painful, and nearly overwhelmed her. The voice went on, pleading, and she knew the speaker. It was Robert, her husband, who for some reason she thought was dead. But no, that was their *ara'sana*. That was Holm, taken by the silver Faceless swarm, dead and gone.

"Alicia," said Robert. "Please."

She felt a gentle touch to the side of her face, a soft, warm pressure that stroked her cheek. With that touch, the constant undercurrent of terror receded. Alicia drew a breath, aware that she could see a dim, reddish glow. Light through closed eyelids. It was a moment before she could remember how to open her eyes, but at last she managed, blinking as a world of faintly colored blurs seemed to swirl around her. They steadied, but remained unfocused, and Alicia realized there were people leaning over her. She counted three of them, although she could see nothing in detail. Having succeeded in a small way with her eyes, Alicia reached for her voice. That worked, but not nearly as well her eyes.

"Rob?" she whispered. She wondered if she had even spoken aloud.

"Here, my love," he replied. "I'm right here."

She still couldn't focus her eyes, but her ears worked well enough, and she could tell from his voice that Robert was crying. Her mind sent the command to raise her arm, but her body did not respond. The weariness filled her with irresistible dead weight and held her firmly in place.

"Don't try to move just yet," said another familiar voice, although this one she could not at first identify. There was a flute-like, musical quality over and behind the words she heard in her head. A voice being translated. It was a soothing, pleasant sound. Not Human, she was sure of that much, and she was vaguely irked that she couldn't recall the name for those with such voices. The flute voice spoke again, with Human words sliding through it from the translation system, providing meaning. "You have been asleep for a very long time. Now you must be at ease and rediscover yourself."

"How? Long?"

There was a pause before she received a reply from Robert. "Just short of two years."

"Oh." That made no sense at all, so she turned her attention to a more immediate and pressing concern. "Am I blind?"

"Not at all," said the flute voice. "Your vision will recover, perhaps in only a few more minutes. Like the rest of you, your eyes have had nothing to do for all this time."

Alicia had the feeling it should all make sense. The flute voice certainly seemed to think so. Having no choice, she did as it suggested and let the weight of exhaustion have its way with her. There was no fighting it. She felt a hand clasp one of hers, and made a feeble effort to return the pressure she felt. It was a warm hand, and familiar. "Rob?"

"Right here."

"You're safe?"

"Yes," he replied. "We all are, now."

"But not Holm." She'd have said that in a whisper regardless of her vocal condition.

Robert didn't answer right away, and had trouble saying the words when he did. "No," he said. "We lost Holm. Our *ara'sana* is gone."

And young Sylvia, she knew, among so many others. But Alicia said nothing more about who had lived and died, remembering then the reason for the pain and the light, the rage and the grief. These feelings were mere echoes of themselves, now, and somehow had something to do with her weariness. She let her thoughts drift elsewhere, unwilling to go to the place in her mind that contained such memories, and this seemed strangely easy to do. Almost as if that place were missing. Thoughts came of others she cared for. “Melep?” she asked. “The children?”

“I am here,” said another much-loved voice. Her free hand was taken into another warm grip, and there was Melep, her *eli’sana*, leaning over her, warm cinnamon in coloring, with a thick mane of black hair. “I am well, as are the children.”

Alicia realized her vision was, indeed, clearing. She felt tiny, smooth scales slide under her fingers as Melep’s grip tightened on her hand. “Two years?” Alicia murmured. “They must have grown.”

“Considerably,” Melep replied. It sounded as if she were laughing and crying at the same time. “Ah, *eli’sana*! It is so good to hear your voice again.”

Alicia found some strength in her hands, and just managed to weakly squeeze those she held. “I want to go home,” she said. “I want to know what happened.”

“Soon,” said the flute voice. An ebony face, thin and angular, with a crest of stiff hair at the crown, loomed over her and came more or less into focus. Beyond, she could easily make out Robert and Melep. “The nanomed is restoring quiescent systems at a respectable pace. You should be ambulatory in a day or two.”

There was a name for that face, now. “Tuleselan.” Her Nesvama colleague and friend.

"Yes, my friend. I am Tuleselan."

"He made it his personal mission to oversee your recovery," Robert said.

"And did a damn fine job of it," said another female voice, one Alicia was sure she did *not* know. A fourth face appeared, youthful, pretty, with bright blue eyes and capped with short blond hair. "I've wondered, at times, why a need was ever seen to bring me in on the case."

"Who...?"

"Dr. Simone Newcomb," said the new voice. "And I'm very pleased to meet you at last, Dr. MacGregor."

"Newcomb?" Fragments of thought associated freely, and matched in part with the name of a shipmind, one that inhabited a probeship she knew to be assigned to this star system. An Artificial she counted as a trusted friend. But no, this was definitely a Human woman. "I don't – know..."

"I'm new here," Dr. Newcomb told her with a smile. "Everyone calls me Doc Simone. Or – just Simone."

"Simone is a neuromed specialist from your Commonwealth," Tuleselan explained. "And she greatly understates her contribution to your recovery. To say nothing of the impending recovery of many others."

To this, Simone simply shrugged, looking slightly embarrassed.

"Are the children here?" Alicia asked.

"No," Robert replied.

"Good," she said. "I'd rather they not see me

like this. Nearly helpless." And was relieved to hear herself speaking in complete sentences, even as speaking wore her out even further.

"That reunion can wait for your homecoming," Melep assured her.

There was a long pause, then Alicia said, "I can't believe this is real. I died. I'm dead. I felt it happen."

"You came very close," Tuleselan admitted. "The powered armor you wore made a difference. The shielding was enough, just enough."

"It was a near thing," Robert agreed, looking grim and tired. "But you made it. And now you're finally awake."

"I am," Alicia said, a warm weight of drowsiness settling over her. "And yet, I'm so very tired. I could sleep. Can we talk more later? I *want* to sleep."

Simone Newcomb made a gesture, and a pale green dataframe shimmered into view. Peering into the display, she nodded. "That's no surprise, really," she said. "You'll drift in and out for a day or so. That's the nanomed sorting out your metabolism, now that we've removed the suppressors and let you wake up."

Alicia would have nodded her understanding, having received medical training along with the rest of her education. But her head didn't seem inclined to move, and her eyes were shutting of their own accord. "Love you," she murmured as she drifted off. "Love you all."

2. Two Years Gone

The next time her eyes opened, Alicia merely felt as if she had roused herself from a deep, perfectly normal sleep. Her vision seemed normal, and looking around she realized she was nestled within a full-support medical module of Commonwealth design. The monitors installed above her head made a soft, almost musical sound every few seconds. That she was in such a pod told her all she needed to know about the seriousness of her condition. And she had been in this pod for the past – *two years?* She shook her head, sure she had heard that wrong. Two years in an induced coma? It was, all by itself, a terrible thing to contemplate. What had the Pulsar device done to her that would take so long to heal?

Two years gone, as if they'd never happened at all. And in a way, for her, that was quite true.

As predicted, she drifted in and out of sleep for another day. With her thoughts ever clearer, she understood the need not to push matters. Alicia relaxed as well as she could under the circumstances. On the third day, and to the relief of Tuleselan and Simone, she truly did experience a normal sleep cycle. With that change came an appetite that would not be satisfied by medications and intravenous supply. A liquid diet was quickly replaced by more solid fare. As her strength returned, she pestered both her attending physicians for information regarding what exactly had happened to her, and how she had been maintained and treated. They were entirely forthcoming, and adamant that it had indeed been two years since her injury.

Two years. It always came back around to that notion, which never seemed less than outrageous. But Alicia was given the records to review regarding her injuries, and studied the summaries of her treatments. There was no choice but to accept the truth they handed her. Her recent life had certainly given her plenty of practice in accepting and dealing with unpleasant truths, however unbelievable they might seem.

Her prior mental health problems had everyone watching her very closely; Alicia didn't hold that against them. Past experiences had badly shaken her equilibrium. She had been a member of the *William Bartram* crew, and was a survivor of that probeship's tragic destruction. She had never been quite the same afterwards. And now, on top of those mental scars was carved the knowledge of that final, desperate fight when the Faceless attacked Pr'pri Star System, seeking a way into the Human Commonwealth.

The scars would have been more painful, but of that battle she could remember nothing to speak of. Her caregivers had seen fit to sequester those memories, tucking them into a locked sector of her memory hoard until she was deemed sufficiently recovered to endure them. This protection did not always spare her the occasional nightmare. Memories of the *William Bartram* disaster had long since been released from sequestration, and dealt with – at least, on a conscious level. Bad dreams based on that terrible time came to her now and then, and did so now as she recovered. One nightmare in particular repeated itself in an unsettling way. She was back aboard the lost *William Bartram*, on the day the great probeship had died. Alicia knew what was coming. She knew they were doomed. But she had lost the power of speech and could not give warning. Alicia woke from these old nightmares covered with sweat, in the grip of deep anxiety. But she knew how to cope with such things; her friend Jeanine Milhouse had taught her well, while helping her through the trauma caused by the destruction of the probeship.

It took longer than predicted, but by the fifth day out of her coma, the nanomed had fully restored her physical strength and coordination, and Alicia could get about on her own. Tuleselan and Simone agreed that it was time for her to go home.

Alicia embraced them both when she received the news. “Thank you, both of you, for everything,” she said.

Tuleselan bowed a little as Simone said, “Seeing you on your feet makes it all worthwhile. Now, remember to take things slow for a while.”

“I will,” Alicia assured her.

“And just to be safe, I’ll monitor the telemetry from your nanomed system,” Simone said. “If anything needs adjusting, I’ll be in touch.”

“I appreciate that,” Alicia replied. “And I’m glad you’re staying on, by the way. I look forward to getting to know you.”

“Likewise,” said Simone.

Within an hour of the decision to release Alicia, Robert came to fetch her home. Knowing her preferences so well, Robert chose the inner-surface tram system for the trip through the habitat to the Rost’aht-MacGregor residence. The air of the habitat was warm and scented by the life inside this vast inverted world called Bartram, a place named after the lost ship in which she and Robert had met and spent the first years of their marriage. They spoke of that loss, which seemed such a long time past when considering all that had followed. They talked all the way home, with Robert filling her in on the many events and changes she had missed. Some of what he had to say came with a certain hesitation, but that revelation only made Alicia smile and shake her head. She kissed him and told him he was being foolish, and the truth was she loved him and Melep too much to be jealous of the nights they'd spent together.

"Of course you did," she said as they passed through a mosaic of woods and fields. "You needed each other. Melep needed *you*. I'd be most displeased if you had done anything less for her." Alicia had grown up in a family that consisted of three open marriages; Robert's upbringing was far more conventional. He was quite aware of the difference, and that she had willingly accommodated his comfort zone in such matters all along. But if anything, her words made Robert more self-conscious, not less. Laughing gently, she drew him to her and kissed him, resisting the urge to tease him about the matter.

The tram slid silently along its invisible magnetic rail, making its way straight and steady down the length of the habitat. They passed through fields and orchards, and across several quick, shallow streams. On either side the landscape faded into a distance that curved up and over their heads until it was lost in the mists around the habitat's axial lamp. Alicia was aware of the vastness of this inverted world she called home, but she no longer *felt* it. Not the way newcomers from the Republic often did, where nothing of this scale – a standard habitat in the Commonwealth – had ever been built. For some visitors from the Republic, the interior of Bartram habitat triggered something akin to agoraphobia.

For Commonwealth Humans such as Alicia and Robert, it was just a place to call home.

In time they entered a region of low, rolling hills covered with turf and decorated by flowering shrubs. For a few minutes they had a clear view of a lake surrounded by willows that just brushed the smooth water with their trailing branches. Beside the lake sat an archaic building designed to replicate a 19th-century British country inn. She knew the place well, and envied the people she saw sitting at outside tables. After all, she hadn't had so much as a drop of ale in two years.

But first – home.

Her home.

It didn't feel like a return from a long absence, since Alicia had only consciously experienced the days since her awakening. The words of her husband as he explained the changes she would see, and the feelings they conveyed, created a sense of disconnection. She'd just left home in the morning, and had been away when the attack came, and a few days had passed since then. Now she was simply going home.

That's how it felt, but she knew otherwise, and could see that it was so. As they walked hand-in-hand up the path to their flethouse — a familiar combination of Commonwealth Neo-pueblo and Leyra'an open-platform architectures — she inspected the place carefully. For here, the truth of time passing in her absence was impossible to ignore. She could see that the feathery Leyra'an verdigris trees were taller – much taller, with long strings of blossoms that looked like white orchids. The trees hadn't been mature enough to flower when the Faceless attacked; two years made the difference. Several robust lilac bushes, new to her eyes, flanked the stone-paved path to the front door, and the vines in their family vineyard were thicker and leafier. The kitchen garden had certainly been enlarged; there was no doubt of that, since the original design had been her project. No changes had been made in the structure of the residence, something that came as a relief to her. Alicia focused on the building and tried to leave the obvious changes in her peripheral vision.

The wide, double front doors of the ground floor burst open and two young boys pelted out at her, shouting *"mama'licia!"* at the tops of their lungs. One boy was Human, her son Paul, with her fair complexion and his father's dark brown hair. At least, it had been dark; she could see fine threads of auburn streaking through it, evidence of her red-headed maternal contribution. The other boy was Vurn, a Leyra'an dark-scaled and sturdy, as his father had been, broader shouldered than Paul. And now she could believe in her heart that two years had been lost to her, and that broke her heart even as she dropped to her knees and gathered the boys into her embrace. They had been six years old the last time she'd held them, born just days apart. They were eight years old now, and looked it. Two years of their lives she had not shared — lost — no matter how many long years stretched ahead for those with the nanomed living inside them.

It was not a change she could consign to the edges of her vision.

Gaia, but it hurt, realizing in her gut finally what two years meant. *Two years*. For people who could live for centuries – no one really knew how long yet – childhood was such an ephemeral thing. Over and done in a flash. Don't blink, or you'll miss it. Alicia had blinked, all unwilling, and her boys had *grown*. She started to cry, and the boys tightened their grip on her, saying words they thought would comfort her. Alicia accepted that comfort, assuring them she would be all right.

Behind them, in the doorway, stood Melep, dressed as Alicia was, Leyra'an style – a long skirt of deep red and a sleeveless blouse of rich green. Under other circumstances, Alicia would have teased her *eli'sana* about the matching colors they wore. Instead, she was caught by the sight of the child, clad in blue overalls, nestled in Melep's arms. The youngster watched the reunion with the boys with wide-eyed wariness. She put one finger in her mouth, suddenly the very picture of two-year-old uncertainty. Like Vurn, she was darker than the average Leyra'an, but in her features looked very much like the woman who held her. She could only be the daughter of Melep and Holm, not yet born when Alicia had seen Melep flee Pr'pri System with the boys and their friend, a young girl named Jaxi. Sent, so they hoped, out of harm's way. The child Melep held was Alicia's *isi'sani,* a Leyra'an word for a child that was not of her bearing, but was her daughter nonetheless, just as the boy Vurn was her son. Born while Alicia slept her unnatural slumber, and now a child of two years.

Alicia scrubbed tears away and forced herself to breath calmly. She stood and, with a boy holding each hand, calmly walked toward her home. "And who is this pretty girl?" she asked, trying very hard to keep her voice from trembling.

"That's Sylvia," said Paul.

"She's our little sister," Vurn added.

Sylvia. Alicia glanced at Robert and saw sadness mirrored there that dwelt in her own heart. Sylvia Milhouse, one of the heroes of the Faceless War, killed protecting those fleeing to shelters beneath the Sibling Species Institute. The same duty that had nearly killed Alicia as well. Sylvia had fallen to the Faceless just before Holm was lost and she herself had – not quite died. There was a holographic memorial outside the SSI, or so she was told, with the images of Sylvia and her newlywed husband William standing their ground. Alicia hadn't been to the SSI since her revival, and honestly wondered if she would be strong enough to look upon those images. They had been so beautiful, Sylvia and William, so young and full of promise, and with so many years ahead of them. They were family, in all the ways that mattered.

“Melep’s choice,” Robert said in a low voice.

“And a good one,” Alicia said. She smiled at the little girl and said, “Hello, Sylvia. I’m so very glad to meet you, *isi’sani.*”

Sylvia turned and buried her face in Melep’s shoulder. “She is rather shy around…” And suddenly averted her gaze, clearly embarrassed.

But Alicia just smiled a little Leyra’an smile, displaying no teeth, and said, “Strangers? But that’s just what I am, *eli’sana*. A stranger. A story you’ve told her of someone she would one day meet.”

“It will take a little time,” said Melep, hugging Sylvia.

“Time.” Alicia took in the sight of her *eli’sana* and the child she held, and sighed. “That’s just fine, now that we can spend that time together.”

3. Home

The household han'anga named Gava'mi didn't share little Sylvia's hesitation. The instant Alicia stepped through the door into the spacious front room, the Beast was on her. Colors rippled and flashed from his crest as it opened like a fan over the back of his head, in bright contrast to his dark, scaly bulk. He capered about, whistling and warbling in the shrill voice of a han'anga both happy and excited, almost knocking her down in his enthusiasm. Even as Robert admonished the silly creature and reached to pull him back, Alicia crouched to gather the scaly reptiloid into her arms. Gava'mi bowled her over then, licking her face as he crawled on top of her. Everyone was laughing, including Sylvia.

"*Now* I feel like I've come home," she said, struggling to her feet, something not made easier by the way Gava'mi pressed his shoulder against her knee. "The Beastie still remembers me."

"Of course he does," said Melep. "And now this place *feels* like home again."

She couldn't wrap her arms around all of them at once, but Melep was in easy reach and had set Sylvia down; the child looked up at them, one arm looped around Gava'mi's stout neck. A heartbeat later the two women were holding each other, crying.

"It must have been hard," Alicia whispered when she could speak.

"It was, *eli'sana*," Melep replied, her voice rough with emotion. "Gods of all clans, I was so afraid you would never come back to us. Or that – you..." Again, she abruptly stopped speaking.

"Wouldn't *really* come back?" Alicia asked. "Not be myself, and whole?"

"There were concerns," Melep said, in something more like her normal voice.

"So I've been told," Alicia replied. "Robert filled me in, on the way home. He, ah, gave a very complete account of the household in my absence."

Melep drew back, her gaze shifting to Robert, then back to Alicia. "Did he, now?" she asked. The scales around her eyes were still darkened by her recent tears.

"Yes." Alicia met the other woman's gaze. "He did. Everything." And leaned forward to press her forehead against Melep's in what for the Leyra'an was a kiss. "It's not a problem, *eli'sana.*"

"I am so relieved to hear that," Melep said. Her eyes shifted for a moment to where Robert stood near the open door, not quite out of earshot. "I gave him very little choice in the matter, though it still took some time for him to accept being *na'ma iff.*"

"How long?" *Na'ma iff*, a borrowed man, and a thoroughly Leyra'an concept. Alicia fought back a sudden urge to giggle when she saw her husband's face redden.

"Four months after Sylvia's birth," Melep replied.

"He's a little slow to figure things out, sometimes," Alicia said in a quiet, conspiratorial way. They looked at each other for a moment, then both suddenly burst out laughing, clinging to each other. Alicia looked over Melep's shoulder to Robert, meaning to explain the outburst, but he held up one hand and shook his head.

"Never mind," he said. "Some things I *can* figure out for myself."

"Eventually," Alicia conceded, to which Robert merely shook his head, though he also smiled.

"Some things will return to normal," Melep said. "At least, so I assume."

"We'll work that out, sweetie, the two of us," Alicia replied.

"Do I get a vote?" Robert asked.

"No," Melep and Alicia replied in unison, then laughed again when Robert rolled his eyes.

They stood for a moment in a companionable silence, then Alicia said, “Could I have a few minutes on my own?”

“Of course,” Melep replied.

Alicia smiled at her family, then wandered through the house, climbing the spiral stair in the heart of the residence to the uppermost exterior family platform. The verdigris trees spread their branches, with their feathery bronze and green foliage, over the wide deck, shading the table and chairs there. The trees truly were thicker and taller than she remembered, and the trailing strings of their blossoms gave the air a faint, sweet scent, an aroma that reminded her of honey. The poles that rose from the perimeter railing still supported the colored Leyra’an crystal lamps that Humans had dubbed elf lights. She walked around to her favorite chair, near a corner of the wide, wooden dining table, trailing her hand over the back of it.

Alicia remembered that on the day of the Faceless incursion she had been here, eating breakfast and drinking *mi’pat* with Robert and Holm; Melep and the children had already evacuated to the Eriola System by then. They’d been deeply worried about the lack of progress the allies were making in the war against the Faceless. Also desperately worried about their friend John Knowles, commander of a relief force rushing to aid the Human Republic; nothing had been heard from him for some time. Only yesterday, it seemed, they worried that the war might one day come here, to their star system. Their home.

Later that very day it had done just that, in a manner no one could have expected, and for a second time in her life Alicia had witnessed the deaths of people she loved. Rost'aht Holm, Sylvia, and William. Just a few days ago – no, two *years* ago.

Two years.

She sat suddenly and awkwardly into the chair, hands over her face. Unbearable grief had her by the throat, and she could barely breathe. Being here, where things were at once familiar and yet changed, made it all so horribly *real*. Holm was truly *dead*. He had lost everything, and they had lost him. And Sylvia, so damned brave and *young*. Alicia scrubbed the tears from her face, suddenly angry with herself, though she couldn't say why, reeling as one emotional surge replaced another.

There was a soft sound behind her. It was the quiet scuff of her *eli'sana's* slippered foot as Melep stepped away from the head of the stair. Melep paused, then came forward, followed closely by Robert.

"We would be more respectful of your wish for privacy," Melep said quietly. "But my heart tells me we should not leave you alone for very long." She made no visible reaction to Alicia's distraught appearance; Melep was not one to belabor the obvious. She took the seat opposite Alicia, while Robert sat beside his wife. The chair at the head of the table, Holm's chair, was almost assertive in its emptiness.

"I keep trying to believe I've been out of it

for so long," Alicia said, her voice little more than a harsh whisper. "Two years," and she shook her head. "I mean, I believe what people are saying, but I can't *feel* it. If that makes sense."

"It does," Robert said. "It makes perfect sense. All of us who survived the war feel something like that, about some aspect of it. We know these horrible things happened. We *saw* them happen." He tapped the side of his head, "It's all here, memories of that terrible reality. But accept it in your heart?" He was looking at the empty chair. "I can't. Even with two years to work on it." Robert sighed and closed his eyes, jaw clenched. "I never will," he said after a pause.

"Acceptance is so easy to suggest, all too easy," Melep conceded. "I lost my husband, and my uncle."

"Ersha?" Alicia felt the tightness return to her chest. "No! Oh, Melep..."

"He and Maladar were in the Republic's capital when the Faceless attacked it," Robert said. "I meant to tell you about that on the way home, but the trip wasn't long enough to cover everything. We're not sure what actually happened. Maladar survived, but Ersha was killed."

Alicia took his hand and held it tight, trying to find the breath to speak again. "Is Maladar here? In Bartram?"

"Not any more," Robert replied. "She came here for a few months, and then joined a Grand Concordance expedition out into the T'lack realm, where they hope to prevent a civil war between two rival factions."

"Gaia!"

Melep watched and listened from where she sat. During a family gathering around this table she would have been in the chair at the other end, the seat of the family matriarch. The Human word did not reflect the Leyra'an meaning of Melep's place in the household; it was not an inherited role. However it was defined, Melep wore it well, but now sat before them signaling a conversation between them as equals. Not that House Rost'aht-MacGregor had often stood on formality. A quiet sort of authority had been the way of Holm and Melep. "No, none of this is easy to accept. And yet acceptance must happen, or the past will surely overwhelm us," Melep told them. "I understand what you say, both of you. But I have worn the gray of mourning, and then set it aside. It was time." She gave Alicia a wry smile and added, "Robert was not the only one slow to embrace the obvious." She nodded toward the empty chair. "It was very hard to move on with life, afterwards."

"I can certainly understand that," said Alicia.

"So we were both – hesitant," Melep admitted.

"So long as it wasn't out of concern for my sake," Alicia said.

"Well, that figured into it," Robert admitted with a shrug. "How could it not?"

"After all, we remained two separate

couples all the while," said Melep. "There was never really a need, but it felt like the right way to be."

"It did," Alicia said. "And it worked perfectly."

"And now we need a new way to make the family hold together," Melep said. "Vurn and Sylvia are the blood of Rost'aht, and so the future of Rost'aht, apart from other concerns, is secure. One day, my son will take his father's place in that chair. Gods willing, he will live to see that day, and raise children of his own. As for me, well, I – have no desire to remarry, you see." Her gaze shifted to Robert, and then back to Alicia.

"I would feel the same way, if I lost *him*," Alicia told her, with a brief glance at Robert. "And if the arrangement that comforted you both was satisfactory, I see no need for you to do so."

"So, what is to be done?" Melep asked.

"It seems simple enough to me," Alicia replied. "A larger bed must be acquired."

"Agreed." And Melep gave her that Mona Lisa smile that was so true to the Way of Leyra'an.

They both looked at Robert.

Who shrugged again. "Do you expect me to object? Seriously, none of the beds in this house are anywhere near big enough."

It was not at all the response Alicia expected, and the laugh that escaped her expressed that surprise. Melep joined her as the laughter took on a life of its own, while

Robert simply looked from one to the other, red-faced yet again, but not looking at all unhappy.

4. Missing Pieces

The changes in and around her home were mostly small things, little more than rearrangements of items that had been there before, with the occasional addition. Little things, but details that added up to an unsettling sense of not being fully connected to her normal life. But then, the life that it seemed she'd left only days ago wasn't really there; it couldn't be. What she found around her reflected that life, an echo from what did not feel like the past, but that reflection was distorted in subtle ways. It was those little things that undermined her efforts to accept and adapt to larger matters: children suddenly two years older than when she had last seen them, a new child who still watched Alicia warily, and the painful absence of Holm – all of these prevented anything like normal life from being truly restored.

Acceptance was the heart of the Way of Leyra'an; that lifeway had long since become hers, and so through it a new life based on the old would develop. She was sure of this, and yet Alicia went through the first days after her release from the hospital fighting to enter a stable orbit, unable to fully accept that these changes could be real.

She returned to her work at the Sibling Species Institute two weeks later, not knowing what to expect. The changes there, in a two-year span, were sure to be significantly greater that those at home. She was already aware that the SSI staff in place at the time of the fighting had been at their work, seeking answers to the Faceless threat, when the enemy arrived. The attack had come so quickly, forcing the use of the untested weapon, that few had made it to hardened shelters in time. The SSI had lost much of its staff that day. Knowing this and seeing it would, she fully expected, be very different things.

The trip by tram took her through a part of the habitat that appeared entirely unchanged. This was a balm for her soul. It all looked and felt so normal; the inner world of the Bartram habitat even *smelled* unchanged. But upon her arrival, it was immediately obvious that the normality she craved was not to be found at her place of employment.

Acceptance. It was so easily said.

The complex looked unchanged. Physical damage from the battle that had taken so much from her, while nearly ending her own life, was gone, repaired soon after the abrupt end of the war. Not a trace of it remained. Alicia had an awkward moment, seeing this. It was almost as if the entire affair had been some sort of hallucination from which she was now awakened. Or a story told to her by someone else. But as she walked into the compound, with its garden of flowers and shrubs from many different worlds, she found the holosculpture of her young friends. Warned by Robert that the memorial existed, Alicia hadn't asked him what it looked like. Nor had she called up images. Now they stood before her, an image taken from records that had survived the battle. They were young, clearly frightened, but resolute in their determination to face this enemy none of them truly understood. To hold back the Faceless until others, just as frightened, had reached the shelters beneath the Institute. Sylvia and William had not flinched in the face of the enemy. Their courage had cost them everything.

Ah, Gaia, but it hurts so much to see you, knowing you're gone.

Alicia fought the urge to hurry past the moment. Her young friends hadn't flinched. Neither would she. Acceptance. It could be done, although it was so often a difficult thing to accomplish. Alicia touched her heart and held that hand out to the memorial. A Gaian thing, from her long-ago childhood. And when had she begun to believe in such things again?

The feeling of disconnection grew painfully

sharp when she entered the Institute through its wide, open doors. The building simply seemed to merge with the garden in the courtyard. It was, as usual, a busy place, brightly lit; this much was perfectly normal. Alicia glimpsed members of all the Sibling Species going about the business of the SSI. Most were Human and Leyra'an wearing a mix of styles from the Commonwealth and the Confederation. Most of the Leyra'an also wore the braided, tri-color sash called *es'ava*, to display their clan affiliations. Great, hulking Hroom strode by with fur of brown, rust, or black, all of them bare-chested and wearing the loose purple trousers and suspenders that would always make them seem, to her eyes, like beings from a child's storybook. With them were diminutive Grahlin, barely a meter tall and all identical, being clones. Their gray coveralls were decorated, shoulder to hip on one side, with bright blue designs that identified their clone lines. A tall, slender Nesvama paused and bowed to her, ebony black with a crest of white hair, and dressed in shimmering robes of pale green. Alicia returned the bow, although she did not recall meeting this Nesvama before.

There were even a few Rusalas, yellow-skinned and wearing what looked more like paint than garments. And a T'lack, insectoid, tall, and most definitely not a Sibling Species, though certainly no less welcome for all of that.

So many people, so many faces, just as it had been before. Except – it was, at the same time, *all wrong*. Alicia felt she was in a living jigsaw puzzle from which many pieces were missing – or had been replaced by pieces that did not fit, and were forced into place. *Faces* were missing, the faces of people she had greeted every day for the first half decade of the Institute's existence. Everyone she passed smiled and welcomed her return, the Leyra'an and the Nesvama with courtly bows, each smiling after the manner of their own kind. But the faces were new, unfamiliar. They truly didn't fit the puzzle she wanted so badly to put together again, knowing all the while that she would never do so.

She went through the motions, meeting and greeting, sometimes tearfully when the meeting *was* with a familiar face, a fellow survivor. That happened all too rarely, and the tears were shared more often than not, all of the Sibling Species having in common the ability to weep. Each time, Alicia was sure it would be the last time she would tear up; she was determined in this matter. And then there would be another.

Mercifully, she experienced very little of the hero worship Robert had endured. He had said little of the matter, but Melep had made it plain that being the man who had destroyed the Faceless quickly became a burden. No matter how often he reminded people that he had not been in that last fight alone, that more than a thousand people in dozens of ships had died to give him his chance to strike, Robert Rost'aht-MacGregor was The Man.

"I'm not surprised," Alicia had told Melep when all had been explained. "He's too gentle a soul to be that kind of hero."

At Alicia's request, no meetings were set for the day of her return to the SSI, and certainly no welcome ceremony – she couldn't have endured such a thing. Tuleselan had been more than happy to comply with her wishes. Alicia made her way to her cherished top-floor office, with its view of the wooded parkland around the institute, but stopped short of entering. The door opposite hers was the entrance to that of her colleague Tuleselan, who had managed the SSI in her absence. From the records she had scanned so far, it was clear not even Alicia could have done better. As a result, there was a rather uncomfortable matter she needed to be sure of, and it was not a thing she should put off. She touched the door chime, knowing the system would announce her presence to Tuleselan. A moment later, the door opened.

"Alicia," he said, rising to his feet and bowing as he clasped his hands together over his chest. His crest of hair was pale lavender, matching the shimmering robe he wore. "I am so glad to see you well enough to return and resume your normal function."

"That remains to be seen," she said quietly, returning his gesture – the standard greeting of Concordance citizens. Grand Concordance, they called it now, having incorporated the Leyra'an, the Humans of the Commonwealth, and a substantial number of Humans from the

Republic. "My return to the position of chief administrator, I mean."

"Ah," said Tuleselan, followed by the tiny warble of a Nesvama mildly surprised. "Please, sit," he said, waving a long-fingered black hand to one of the chairs in front of his oval desk. "Coffee?"

"I'd like some, thanks."

They both sat, and Tuleselan tapped several keys on the pad set into his desk. In a structure bearing an Artificial, such as the probeship currently parked in Pr'pri System, he would have spoken the request aloud and coffee would have been sent. But the Bartram habitat was not yet inhabited by a mature Artificial, although a clone had been installed, according to Robert; such things often took time to grow into full function. That the habitat had been constructed without an artificial intelligence at its heart was a holdover from the days when negotiations with the Republic required a venue in accordance with the Republic's laws forbidding AI. Alicia had once considered this a strange sort of bigotry until its origin was revealed to be the result of the Republic's own misuse of such technology.

The Bartram habitat was sufficiently automated that the coffee service appeared from the wall less than a minute later, sliding onto the sideboard built there to accommodate such deliveries. Tuleselan rose in haste, as if afraid Alicia would serve herself, or worse, serve them both. The Nesvama prided themselves on being exemplary hosts, and such a thing simply would not do. Knowing this, Alicia sat tight, suppressing a smile, allowing her friend to follow the ways of his people.

"When did you start drinking coffee?" she asked as he poured himself a cup, as well. Alicia knew caffeine worked the same for Nesvama as for Humans and the Leyra'an, but… "I thought you couldn't abide the taste of it?"

"I've learned that, with sufficient adulteration, it can be enjoyed." And he had indeed dosed his liberally with cream and a pale, pinkish powder Alicia couldn't identify.

"That may be one change too many for me," Alicia said, taking hers black, as always. She even managed to laugh with him, briefly, at her own jest.

They sipped coffee for a moment, and after that moment she said, "It was such a relief to see you there, when I woke up. You must have been away from the habitat when the Pulsar was detonated."

"My mate and I were on our way back from a visit home when the enemy arrived. Two days out from the Eriola nodal point. Still, we were close enough to feel the effects. They were most unpleasant, but we were unharmed." He took another sip, holding the mug between his hands. "The Nesvama proved unusually resistant to the side effects of the weapon. Unlike the Grahlin."

Alicia grimaced and nodded, but didn't belabor the obvious. When the trans-dimensional disruptor – nicknamed the Pulsar

– had been detonated, in a final desperate attempt to halt the advance of their enemy, the Grahlin population of Bartram had been nearly wiped out. Only those in the hardened shelters had survived, although they didn't emerge unscathed. "To say nothing of the original staff of the Institute," she said instead.

"Yes," he whispered, the word in his own language – translated in her ear – a downward slurred whistle. "We have been all of the past two years rebuilding and refilling empty positions among researchers and support staff. As a result, we have only just begun to pick up the threads of disrupted research projects. It has been – very hard."

"I can only imagine," she replied. "But I've been sorting through your reports on SSI administration, and I am, frankly, deeply impressed. What you have accomplished, my friend, especially considering your circumstances, is nothing less than extraordinary."

"I did not work alone," he pointed out with typical Nesvama modesty.

"No, but those who have assisted you were selected *by* you," Alicia said. "So my praise is hardly misplaced."

"I do appreciate that," said Tuleselan. "But now *you* have been restored, and have returned to us."

"Do I understand you to be eager to step down from the Director's position?"

"You do," he replied. "I have done my best to restore order and function, but such duties do not suit me."

"I ask, because if you *want* to keep this position, you have earned it," Alicia said. "I would willingly take on some other function."

"I appreciate that as well," he said, seeming slightly agitated, revealed by the way he twisted and turned the mug around between his fingers, a fidgety sort of gesture. Alicia knew then that Tuleselan wanted very much to hand the Director's duties back to her. "But I believe you are a better administrator, so it is in the best interests of the Institute to have you resume your former position."

Alicia chose her next words with care. In truth, she wanted to be back in the proverbial saddle, but Tuleselan certainly deserved better than simply being set aside. That he actually wanted to relinquish the position made things easier. "I appreciate the sentiment. But would you consider stepping sideways instead of stepping down?"

"Sideways?"

"I'm going to need so much help getting up to speed," she said with a wry smile. "That means *your* help, as SSI co-director. Otherwise it would take me about as long to catch up as I've been out of action."

"A temporary position, then," Tuleselan said. "And you underestimate your abilities."

"Yes, temporary. And no, I surely don't."

"That arrangement is most acceptable." He sipped his coffee.

"Thank you, my friend," she said with a sigh of relief. "Now, the reports I've been scanning show our top priorities as the fate of the Godsend Star System, and the *Surnia* download."

"You are in agreement with those decisions?" Tuleselan asked.

"Completely." She leaned back in the chair, holding her mug between her hands in her lap. "Although it would seem we have very few options regarding Godsend, apart from watching and waiting."

"Yes. When the Faceless shifted its Radiant here from Godsend, both its gravimetric nodes destabilized and then completely collapsed. Probes we send there are not heard from again. We have stopped sending probes."

"Do we have any idea how long it will be before nodal stability restores itself?" she asked. "The material I've reviewed is less than forthcoming on the matter."

"We cannot make direct measurements of the system, so accurate calculations cannot be made," Tuleselan pointed out. "Sending a probe through real space would take more than three hundred standard years."

"It's so easy to forget how big the universe really is," Alicia said. "Using the trans-spacial nodes into the matrix, we quickly take it for granted that the vastness between stars is no longer relevant."

"Indeed."

"Care to guess what sort of wait we might have?" she asked.

"You no doubt recall that both the Rusalas and Nesvama experienced Radiant relocations," Tuleselan said. When she nodded, he said, "Based on events involving stellar systems of comparable mass and classification, I would say we will all be at least eighteen years older before we visit the Godsend System. That is an optimistic projection. I have seen other estimates that approach five decades."

"That's quite a spread."

"The complicating factor is that of distance. In the past, the farther the Faceless Radiant shifted, the greater the distortion that occurred when it left and then re-entered real space-time. The effect is much stronger at the point of departure, which is why we were merely and briefly inconvenienced here. The shift from Godsend to Pr'pri is more than sixty times the greatest distance previously recorded."

"So, off the scale," Alicia muttered.

"Yes, and it is also why we were so taken by surprise. There was no way to know the Faceless could perform such a relocation." He gave an almost Human shrug of narrow Nesvama shoulders. "Where before systems have been closed for a few years, we now have a situation in which decades may pass."

"Gaia," she whispered, shaking her head. "So we can only hope the natives were left unmolested by the Faceless."

"It is possible the Faceless ignored them. The natives of Godsend had a pre-industrial society, from what little we've been able to learn." He repeated the shrug. "And that is very little indeed."

Alicia nodded and finished her coffee,

aware of these few details and how they had been obtained, without recourse to her memory hoard. Before the invasion of Pr'pri System, a damaged warship had limped into Pr'pri early in the war, bearing a handful of men who had been in the Godsend System when the Faceless first arrived there. They had been several years lost between the stars. Their records and recollections had made the allies aware that Godsend – originally a base for renegades from the Republic – contained an inhabited living world, peopled by primitive agrarians. That was all they had to go on. "This *Surnia* download, the one Rob came home with, may contain data on the matter," she said. She'd seen a report, and then heard the story of Robert's encounter with the captive Artificial that once had been a shipmind. The Faceless had tried to assimilate it, but failed, leaving it able to resist the enemy behind the scenes.

With a warble that stood for a derisive laugh in his species, Tuleselan said, "The download could contain almost anything. The Artificials are still trying to find a way to unpack it."

"Artificials can't open it?" she asked. "Gaia! It must be seriously corrupted."

"I am not sure mere data corruption is the problem," Tuleselan replied. "The Faceless fought the download process as it was happening. It would appear that it may have been all too successful. But we have not been able to analyze enough of what the *Surnia* carries to be sure."

"It's still *in* the *Surnia*," Alicia observed. "I saw that in the report and was puzzled by it."

"Yes. It is somehow locked in the ship's memory. All attempts at downloading it to the Library Annex have been fruitless."

"The *Surnia's* Artificial can't help from its position inside?"

"The Artificial mind of that ship appears to be quite dead."

"Oh." That information hadn't been included in the overview she'd scanned. The thought of such an entity being extinguished gave her a shudder. If there was a more benign form of life in the Universe...

"But we continue to study the matter," Tuleselan assured her. "We may well succeed in the end, and one day we will fully understand the calamity that took so much from us all."

She nodded in agreement. What Robert had been told by the shipmind of the lost probeship *Henrietta Leavitt* gave them the basic story of the Faceless and its origins, but it was merely an outline of what the *Leavitt* had wanted them to know. "I hope we succeed, if only to ensure that the Artificial who gave up its own life on our behalf didn't die in vain."

"Indeed, yes," said Tuleselan.

They moved on to the long list of current projects, most of which had been begun under her guidance and were just now moving forward again. Alicia had already updated her standard and still functional memory hoard – what was to be done with the ruined auxiliary hoard had yet to be determined – but talking about such data always made for easier access at a later date. In due time she made her way to her own office, and smiled when she saw that the staff had somehow kept her cluttered home-away-from-home clean, without moving a single item a centimeter from where she had left it. Considering how many items filled the room – paintings on walls, old-style paper books, shelves holding specimens, and even a few toys left behind when her children visited – it was an impressive accomplishment. She might have just left it the day before, not two years ago.

Two years.

Alicia sat behind her desk with a weary sigh and bowed her head.

This feels too much like what happened after the Bartram disaster. I don't want to go through that again.

She was, at least, spared any risk of reliving her last memories of the battle, in her sleep or otherwise. A compartment of her functional memory hoard was locked up, containing as it did the sequestered memory of the fight that had killed Holm, Sylvia, and Will. Simone Newcomb wanted other aspects of Alicia's health, mental and physical, completely stable before unlocking that compartment. Alicia was in no hurry. Knowing three she loved so dearly had been killed was hard enough. The thought of remembering the event, seeing it happening in her mind's eye, frankly appalled her. And so Alicia hadn't argued the point, remembering as she did how useful memory sequestration had been when dealing with the aftermath of the Bartram disaster.

Alicia also knew there were risks in keeping traumatic memories sequestered for too long. The technique was meant to support therapy, not replace it. She wasn't anywhere near being ready to recall clearly what had happened, but she never would be without taking certain first steps. Alicia could see no point in waiting to start that therapy. Now was the time to lay the groundwork. She summoned a bright green dataframe from the habitat's communication system. "Comm, Alicia MacGregor to Dr. Jeanine Milhouse."

"Hello!" a familiar female voice said a moment later when contact was made. "Hey, we heard you were finally awake and home." The dark-haired woman looking back at her from the dataframe gave her a smile. "It's so good to hear you. See you. What took you so long and when are we all getting together to celebrate?"

Alicia couldn't help smiling back at her friend, even as she noted the weary look in the woman's eyes. The mother of young Sylvia might live for centuries with Commonwealth nanomed in her body, but she did not wear the past two years well. "Very soon, to hear Rob and Melep talk. Probably at the Willow Lake. But I need to see you before then."

"Oh?"

"Yes. It would seem I need your help. Again."

5. Heal Thyself

An hour later, Alicia sat on a bench in the park that surrounded the SSI, her arm around Jeanine's shoulders. The other woman slumped forward as if exhausted by the weight of some great burden. Feelings of guilt and embarrassment vied for priority in Alicia's already mixed emotions. "I really should have thought before I suggested meeting there."

"Not your fault, my dear," Jeanine said. She sighed and shook her head, leaning forward with her arms on her knees. Long, black hair hid her face, but the sadness in her voice made her state of mind all too obvious. "I knew about the memorial. I've even seen images of it. But the real thing? Life-sized? A different matter. I – well, I thought I could handle it." Another deep sigh was released, and she seemed to shrink down into herself.

The area of the park to which they had retreated blocked their view of the main entrance. Alicia had found her friend out there in the garden courtyard, where they had agreed to meet, standing in front of the memorial to Sylvia and Will, Jeanine's daughter and son-in-law. The designer had left just enough of a translucent character in the holosculpture to make it plain that the viewer was not standing before two living beings. It was still near enough to lifelike to leave Jeanine completely unstrung by the time Alicia got there.

"They meant well," Alicia said. "Those who set up the memorial."

"I certainly don't hold it against them," Jeanine replied quietly. "It's a fine thing, beautiful, and done from love and respect. I'm, ah, rather surprised that nothing similar was done for Holm."

"Not the Leyra'an way," Alicia said. "Melep told me they wanted to include him, but she vetoed the idea. The Leyra'an don't honor the fallen in that fashion."

"Instead, she named her daughter after mine."

"That *is* the way of the Leyra'an," Alicia said. "It's why one of our boys is named Vurn. After a dear friend who died when we lost the *William Bartram*."

"And I don't object to that, either," Jeanine said somewhat hastily, sitting up straight and turning a tearful gaze on Alicia. "That little girl is a rare gem. She wears the name well, and Greg and I couldn't love her more if she were ours."

"I'm glad."

They were quiet for a long, companionable moment, then Jeanine said, "It's an even bet which of us will be counseling the other." And she gave Alicia a trembling smile.

"I'm not going to argue methods," Alicia said.

"I'm serious," Jeanine insisted. "Helping you work through what happened will likely be therapeutic for me. One of the things I frequently need to instill in others is a sense of purpose. A reason to move on. Working with you will surely give me that."

"You haven't been working with others all along?" Alicia asked with a frown.

Jeanine shook her head. "I probably should have, but in my case 'physician heal thyself' was easier said than done. I – haven't done much of anything, at all, these past couple of years."

"Ironic, really," said Alicia. "Considering how much you were able to help survivors of the *William Bartram*. Myself included."

Alicia knew this for an understatement. A significant number of Bartram residents were, like Alicia herself, survivors of the disaster that had befallen the probeship for which the habitat was named. Jeanine had once worked with families in the Republic, those who lost loved ones in the long conflict between that Human nation and the Leyra'an. She'd given up her practice when her husband was stationed in Pr'pri as military escort for the

Republic's representatives to the old Trilateral Peace Talks. First with Alicia, then eventually with many others, Jeanine had found herself drawn back into a new practice. Alicia was only one of dozens of people who had come to grips with the reality of their losses through the help of Jeanine Milhouse.

"I suppose it is," said Jeanine. "And it isn't like I lacked support. Greg gave me his best, and Rebecca has been a rock, even as she struggled to accept the loss of her sister. But I received more than I gave, I'm afraid."

"Rob told me Greg was a mess right after it happened," said Alicia.

"That would be putting it mildly," Jeanine replied. "But your husband got his feet on the right path. Robert has a special quality to him, something that gives hope to others. He said the right things to Greg, and because he did, Greg came home able to keep me on *my* feet." She met Alicia's gaze. "I owe your family a great deal. Melep and Robert were both there for us, always there. They were amazing, considering what they'd both endured. Especially Melep. But having each other surely..." She stopped speaking and cast a quick sidelong glance at Alicia.

"I know all about that." Alicia laughed quietly when she saw the look on Jeanine's face. "Not a concept that works in the Republic, I suppose."

"Well, it would raise eyebrows, to say the least. It doesn't bother you?"

"Not at all," Alicia replied, shaking her

head. "I'd have been quite cross with them if they hadn't taken comfort in each other."

"Your husband and another woman – while you were comatose." Jeanine looked as puzzled as she sounded.

"If it had just been some other woman, I'm not entirely sure how I'd feel about it. But Melep?" Alicia smiled and slowly shook her head. "She's my *eli'sana*. I love her. I'm glad they could be together when it was needful."

"People really are different in the Commonwealth."

"Not so different, really," Alicia replied. "Although it does vary. My family, when I grew up, wasn't quite as – well, let's just say, as traditional as Rob's. It's not that I'm never possessive, but in this case, I'd be that way about them both. Meaning my husband and my *eli'sana*. And Holm, when he was still alive. A double marriage among the Leyra'an doesn't *require* partner sharing, but it's perfectly acceptable behavior for those who are so inclined."

"And now that you're back, I suppose..."

"It's the three of us, now," Alicia said. "It's comfortable."

"The way of the Leyra'an?" Jeanine asked.

"The way of House Rost'aht-MacGregor," Alicia told her. "At least, it is now. Does that trouble you?"

"No, not really," Jeanine said. "The way I was raised, this would be frowned upon, at the very least. But living here has taught me to accept that there are many ways people can live and love and be happy. Greg and I would never be able to manage such an arrangement, but that doesn't mean it can't work for someone else."

"And it does," Alicia assured her. She took her friend's hand and changed the subject. "Look, if this is a bad time..."

"To come back out of retirement?" Jeanine shook her head and said, "Not to help you, it isn't. Besides, like I said, between the two of us, we might *both* get better. There are so many people living here, stuck in that same disconnect you described over the comm. Expecting faces they'll never see again. Counseling them used to be my profession. Hell, it was a calling. I've always believed that, and I still do." She looked vexed. "But the best I've managed so far is to get used to coping with my own grief from day to day. I *need* to move forward. To get back to what made me whole. This will be a good start."

"We should probably talk to Dr. Newcomb about my situation," Alicia said. "From what she's told me, my condition may be complicated by the physical damage associated with my totally blocked memory hoard, as well as the emotional trauma I've endured."

"You no longer have a functioning memory hoard?"

"I have the standard hoard, in which the memory of that last day is sequestered," Alicia replied. "It's the auxiliary model that's messed up. Not everyone has that one."

"That's right, I remember you saying so,"

Jeanine said. "I've heard of Dr. Newcomb, but we haven't met."

"She's made a good impression," Alicia said. "Other people are waking up in as good a shape as I'm in, if not better. Because of her work, I mean."

"I'll definitely want to talk to her," Jeanine agreed. "Get an assessment of the physical damage you endured, and learn what was done in the regeneration process." She smiled and added, "Looks to me like you regenerated just fine. The shorter hair style surprises me, but it suits you."

"Why, thank you, dear." Alicia released Jeanine's hand and brushed at her red hair, laughing a little. "They kept it very short while I was out, but I think I'll let it grow back to what I'm used to."

"You said your auxiliary hoard is, what? Blocked? What did you mean by that?"

"It acts as if it's loaded to capacity, with damage to the data access protocols," Alicia replied. "No one knows how that happened. So there it sits," and she tapped the side of her head, "completely inert."

"I've always wondered why you troubled with the auxiliary hoard," Jeanine said.

"It's not all that unusual," Alicia replied with a shrug. Her own motive for doing so was quite unusual, but she left that matter aside. Only her immediate family knew of the brief conflict that had taken place between her and the Artificials of the Commonwealth, when she discovered the Human heritage encoded in the

Leyra'an genome. "I know several people at the Institute who've found a need for one."

"I see," said Jeanine. "Okay, so give me something of a baseline. How are you coping? Anxiety attacks? Nightmares?"

Alicia nodded and said, "I had some short, disturbing dreams about the *William Bartram* just before the clinic released me. I'm happy to say that there haven't been any more since then. Mostly problems with anxiety, and a tendency to flinch at sudden loud noises. I feel like I can't quite catch my breath, but not in a physical way. Emotional breath, if that makes sense."

"It does," Jeanine replied. "I was that way for several months, afterward. That's only to be expected."

"I'm too easily distracted," Alicia added. "And I, um, cry easily. None of which is normal for me."

"Not normal, no, but not unexpected, all things considered," Jeanine said. "Did anything in particular happen that prompted you to call me?"

"Nothing specific," Alicia admitted. "But – how to say it? There's a growing feeling of anxiety, as if something *is* about to happen. I keep remembering how it was when we lost the *Willie B.* I was grief-stricken, and worried sick over Robert, not knowing whether or not he was still alive. But then he came home and everything seemed fine. I got into a stable orbit and held it."

"Until you boarded the wreck of the

probeship."

"Exactly," Alicia agreed. "And once it was triggered..."

"You're afraid something of the sort will happen this time?"

"Sooner or later," Alicia replied. "My gut feeling is that it's inevitable."

"You said there's a sequestered memory sequence?"

Alicia nodded. "The sequence involving the attack and the deaths I witnessed. Holm's death. Up to and including what I thought was my own demise."

"That explains why you haven't had worse symptoms," Jeanine told her. "Right now, you're in a state of knowing what happened, but not being able to *feel* it."

"And I do remember, from our past work together, that leaving things that way can be risky," said Alicia. "Especially if a strong enough emotion triggers a rupture in the sequestration protocols. That's really the thing I'm most afraid of."

"Which, as I recall, was what caused your crisis aboard the wreck."

"Exactly," Alicia said. "Being there, the protocol broke down and I saw it all happening, while floating there in the dark. Full blown panic attack. In an EVA suit and under null-g. I am, frankly, lucky to be alive."

"No kidding," Jeanine replied. "Who managed the sequestration this time? I'd want them on hand when the memory is released."

"Dr. Newcomb and one of her assistants, a

tech named Sharon Reid," Alicia replied. "One of the few familiar faces I have left in there," she added with a nod toward the sprawling complex beside them. "Sharon worked in the neurobiology sector before the war. We didn't actually know each other, to speak of, but she was still, well, a familiar face."

"When was the memory sequestered?"

"The day I woke up," Alicia replied. "Dr. Newcomb thought it was a wise precaution. She said that during their first attempt to wake me up, I immediately relived the end of that fight. I don't remember that, but my reaction apparently put a scare into poor Robert and Melep. So they locked that pattern up in my functional hoard."

"I should have been there, helping them manage things all along." Jeanine slowly shook her head and sighed. "When the regeneration therapies were being applied to you, I just wasn't up to it. And once I was out of the loop, I just stayed out. Even though your family made it plain my help would be welcome." She looked down, clearly embarrassed.

Surprised by this admission, Alicia twisted on the bench and put her arms around Jeanine again, hugging her. "You had enough to deal with. Don't worry about it. Please."

"Oh, you know me better than that," Jeanine said, returning the embrace. "Of course I'll worry about it."

"True, you will." They sat facing each other for a moment, then Alicia asked, "When do we start?"

"We already have," Jeanine replied with a smile. "But before we really settle into therapy, I'll need to contact Dr. Newcomb. We do need to work together on this. Unfortunately, that won't happen right away."

"Something wrong?" The vexed look on Jeanine's face surprised Alicia.

"I'm not really sure," Jeanine replied, still looking annoyed as she answered. "Greg's family is coming for a visit. Some of the communications we've had with them, well, they really aren't pleased with him for accepting dual citizenship."

"Do I recall correctly that they rejected nanomed tech?"

"You do, indeed," Jeanine replied. "And have openly stated that we are all going to burn in hell for subverting the will of God. Every time they come here, it's one more attempt to 'save' us."

"That should be a fun visit."

With a derisive grunt, Jeanine stood up and said, "We'll start work as soon as I can. Which means as soon as they've gone home. I doubt it's going to be a long visit. But I'll contact Dr. Newcomb before then, get that conversation started."

Alicia stood with her and they embraced again. "Take care of family first," she said. "I don't believe my situation is urgent right now. And – thanks."

"Hey, what I said before? I really do think this will help me as much as it does you."

"I hope so," said Alicia. "I truly do. Because

I already owe you so much."

"And don't hesitate to call me if something starts to slip."

"I won't," Alicia assured her.

They went their separate ways, Jeanine to prepare for unwelcome visitors, Alicia to the Institute and straight to Simone's office. Simone had been offered, and had accepted, a position within the Institute. It had occurred to Alicia that it would be polite to give her a heads up.

6. Simone

The office door was open, so Alicia stepped in. “Hello, Simone. Spare me a few minutes?”

Simone looked up and smiled, saying, “I have no pressing matters calling for my attention at the moment. Come on in.”

The tidiness of Simone’s office was in complete contrast to Alicia’s own, very cluttered, workspace two floors above. In design, the two were identical. The ports for automated delivery systems were in the same locations above the standard sideboard shelf, and Simone’s desk was typical of such, wood-topped over gently curving steel legs – in this case enameled in dark blue – and longer than wide, with input panels set off to one side. The walls were white, the floor carpeted in dark blue to match the desk, before which sat a pair of chairs that matched the decor. The desk was clean, and on the otherwise bare walls were displayed only a pair of 3-D images. One was of a scene looking down the length of a habitat or probeship interior, from the perspective one would have perched inside an end cap. The landscape curved up on each side, vanishing into the bright glare of the axial light. The second was an image of the Human home world, Earth, bright and blue and white against the black Void.

Alicia wondered if Simone truly was a neat and tidy person, or if she simply hadn't been in the office long enough yet to begin accumulating clutter. Then she considered the plain beige, long-sleeved shirt and brown pants the other woman wore, and decided that plain, simple, and orderly were the ways of Simone Newcomb.

There had been a blue-rimmed dataframe in the air between Simone and the door when Alicia stepped in. With a quiet word of command, it was banished, shrinking in an instant to a point of light and then gone. Alicia stepped into the office and sat down.

"You don't look entirely happy," Simone observed.

With a wan smile, Alicia said, "It's been a trying day, coming back to see so many new faces. Knowing *why* there are so many new faces."

"No, I don't suppose that's been at all easy," Simone replied. "I can only imagine how hard it is on you. After all, I've never experienced anything remotely like what you've been through."

"I sincerely hope you never do." Alicia hesitated, then plunged on. "You know I went through a rough time before the war came here."

"From the records I was given," Simone replied with a nod. "And from Robert."

"I've contacted the therapist who helped me get through that," Alicia said. "Jeanine Milhouse. She specializes in cases like mine. Used to practice in the Republic, working with their military to help survivors, especially civilians who had lost loved ones."

"I've heard of Dr. Milhouse," Simone said. "She's well thought of in her field. Tuleselan wanted to recruit her for our team, but she was, well..."

"There was a problem at home, after the war."

"I understand they lost a daughter in the fighting," Simone said.

"The girl in the memorial, out in front of the Institute."

"Oh, yes," Simone said. "I've seen it, and the flowers people leave in front of it."

"She was much loved," said Alicia, then quickly getting back to a slightly less uncomfortable topic. "Jeanine and I just had a talk about her resuming our therapy sessions."

"You're having problems coping, then," said Simone. "That's not unexpected. I've been monitoring your nanomed telemetry, but so far nothing has been flagged as abnormal. What exactly are you experiencing?"

"Nothing that I'd call a crisis, so far," Alicia replied. "Some anxiety. Also, a feeling of disconnection. I feel like I'm not really here, in this world. Everything is familiar and different at the same time, which is as distracting as it is disturbing."

"I expected something of the sort might crop up, considering what you've been through," Simone said. "To be honest, I'm relieved that it isn't much worse than what you describe. I have someone on my team that I had in mind should problems arise, but you've already worked with Dr. Milhouse, so of course I'll abide by your choice. I'm available if you or your friend think I can be of any help."

"Thanks for that," Alicia replied. "I'd really appreciate it if you could work with Jeanine, especially if what happened to me creates any unique situations."

"Happy to oblige," Simone assured her. "I've been working on the assumption that you'd need some help with the fallout from what's happened to you. What you're recovering from is a sort of neurological trauma not previously on record in the Commonwealth. I rather doubt it's possible to be overcautious in your case. I'll assist Dr. Milhouse in any way I can."

"Thanks," Alicia replied. "Jeanine was pretty insistent that you at least be on hand when the sequestered memories are unblocked."

"Except possibly for that," Simone said carefully. "At least, not anytime soon."

"Her methods involve confronting memories of the traumatic experience," Alicia explained. "Talking through them, putting them in the context of life in its entirety."

"Not unlike such counseling in the Commonwealth, with careful manipulation of serotonin, oxytocin, and vasopressin levels," Simone said with a nod of understanding. "The nanomed will do that by generating a mildly psychedelic state, which ordinarily would ease you into that confrontation."

"Yes," said Alicia. "That's how we managed things before."

"Unfortunately, there's a complicating factor. You recall that when we first tried to wake you up, there was a serious problem."

"I was told that I immediately relived those last minutes," Alicia replied. "When I saw Holm die and the weapon was discharged."

"You lived it as if it were real, here and now," Simone said. "The shock unraveled some of the repair work the Nesvama did. After we'd recovered that lost ground, we used existing records to find the point at which we should sequester memories, rather than simply eliminating the dangerous neuropattern."

"Robert said something about that, the day he brought me home," Alicia asked. "That all involved agreed that deletion should be a last resort."

"We did," Simone replied. "In the first place, permanent memory deletion without your consent would have been unethical and, frankly, illegal. Your partners – Melep and

Robert – agreed with me to use sequestration instead. There are too many variables here, your condition being one for which there is no precedent. We're not sure that the problem is insurmountable, so a permanent deletion seemed too drastic." She hesitated, then said, "That can still be done, of course. Your choice."

"How safe is it to leave that pattern in place?" Alicia asked. "Even in a memory hoard? I've had a bad experience with a sequestration breakdown."

"Yes, I saw that in your medical records when I was brought in on the case," Simone said. "Robert, Melep, and I discussed it at some length. There's never zero risk, of course, but with the Hroom improvements made to the sequestration protocols, I believe it's quite safe." Simone smiled a little as she added, "We've already seen that these protocols are more robust than before. With previous techniques, just being in this building would probably trigger a sequestration breakdown. From what you've said, it's apparent that nothing of the sort has happened."

"Not yet," said Alicia. She frowned as a belated thought occurred. "I can't help wondering – wasn't the nanomed system programmed to apply the proper neuropeptide response when you woke me up that first time? By my understanding of these things, that should have prevented what happened."

Simone grimaced and answered first with a curt nod. "It should, indeed, have prevented what happened, or at least mitigated it. We don't yet know why it failed."

"Well, this doesn't exactly go with the plan I was putting together," Alicia said. "So, how do you think we should proceed?"

"Slowly," Simone replied. "And I don't mean to sound flippant in saying that. So long as you don't have anything as serious as panic attacks, we take our time. I'll continue monitoring your situation through the nanomed telemetry while I confer with Dr. Milhouse regarding how and when to remove the sequestration protocol."

Alicia considered all she had been told. "But you'd do it now, if I asked?"

"I'd be on record as advising against it," Simone said. "But ethically, I wouldn't have any right to refuse." Tilting her head a little to one side she asked, "Is this what you *want* me to do?"

Alicia considered the idea for a moment, then shook her head and said, "No, not yet. I wouldn't want the memory erased. Forgetting about what happened wouldn't change anything. And somehow it feels like it would be disrespectful. I need to deal with it, just as I dealt with what happened to the *William Bartram*. From working with her before, I know why Jeanine wants to proceed as soon as possible, but she obviously doesn't realize there's more to this than a traumatic memory. The severity of the physiological and neurological shocks you've worked to repair in me wouldn't occur to her."

"It didn't occur to *anyone*, before your

situation developed," Simone told her. "Scared the hell out of us, the way you came up out of that pod, screaming your head off."

"Robert said it was bad, but he wouldn't elaborate," Alicia said. "I haven't had the heart to push the issue."

"I can't blame him for that," Simone replied. "The details are in your record if you really want to know. Nothing we measured during the incident gives a clue as to why you reacted as you did. The team Tuleselan and I have working on the matter, believe that some confluence of effects from the Pulsar weapon, possibly also due to the proximity of the Faceless itself, altered or augmented the impact of your experience, creating an abnormal memory pattern. Augmented it in a way that made it seem very real to you, and because of that, triggered a *physiological* reaction. A loud one. How close that might be to the truth remains to be seen."

"How many others are so afflicted?"

"We don't know for certain." Simone looked uncomfortable. "Of the many people being treated, you're one of the seven survivors we've been able to revive, so far. Unfortunately, all of you reacted badly, to some degree. Your situation was the worst of them, but you were also the first. It's possible we brought you up too quickly, so we slowed the process with the others. It seemed to help. Anyway, it adds up to less than the success we hoped for, but then, the sample size is too small for solid conclusions."

“I take it further revivals are on hold until we know more?” Alicia asked.

“I’m afraid so,” Simone replied. “I’ll arange a meeting with Dr. Milhouse, and make sure she understands the risk involved with what she would normally do.”

“I appreciate that,” Alicia said. She rose and turned toward the door, then paused, and looked back. “I’ve been told that, when I’m up to it, there’ll be a big celebration at the Willow Lake Inn. Sort of a welcome home party. Pretty sure I’ll be able to handle it soon, and I’d appreciate it if you’d join us.”

“I’ve been to the Willow Lake with Robert and Melep, among others,” Simone replied. “It’s become a personal favorite. Just message me with a day and time. I’ll be there.”

Alicia left Simone’s office and returned to her own, where she spent the rest of the day immersed in the work of catching up on all the SSI activities, concentrating on summaries of a project that had been unfolding before she was caught up in the final battle: work related to the First Iteration message being found in the genetic code of organisms from hundreds of worlds. This project was the primary reason the Sibling Species Institute had been created in the first place. Humans from the original timeline had sent their Artificials back in time to tamper with the biology of these living worlds, which triggered the evolution of the people known as Leyra’an, Hroom, Grahlin, Nesvama, and Rusalas. The universe of space-time proved intolerant of paradox, and so one result of this tampering had been a split in the time line, occurring many millions of years in the First Iteration past. The second, alternate chain of events was the reality in which Alicia and everything she knew and cared about had their existence.

Wherever they'd worked, the people of the First Iteration had left a persistent message in the genetic code, preserved in DNA sequences by a system more complicated than anything Alicia and her colleagues had imagined. She remembered predicting great advances in genomics and genetic engineering due to what they uncovered along the way to translating that message. Summaries on the dataframes that now surrounded her made it very clear that she had seriously underestimated just how great those advancements would be.

She had a lot of catching up to do. The prospect excited her, and so for a time, she forgot her troubles. Another sort of therapy, and one she embraced with a will.

At the beginning of one overview was a clip from the first part of the message, containing a video component that still made her shiver. Everyone living in the Second Iteration time line had a counterpart in that of the First Iteration, but even knowing this, the thought that she might confront her own doppelgänger would never have occurred. And yet, that was exactly what had happened. The Alicia MacGregor of the First Iteration had been the coordinator of the effort that sent Artificials back in time through the multi-dimensional matrix. And so it was that a worn and beaten version of Alicia had addressed them in that video, clothing rumpled and red hair cut very short – as it was on Alicia's head at the moment. Alicia had been well into her therapy with Jeanine Milhouse when that translated bit of message came to light. The shock of seeing and hearing herself explaining what had been done to give Humanity a second chance, while making it plain that Humanity of the First Iteration was doomed, had been terrible – and a significant setback.

The work of the First Iteration had created intelligent species, and as a byproduct, changed the culture of a totally alien species – the T'lack – rendering them capable of taking a more tolerant approach to dealing with other species. The T'lack of this Second Iteration were the friends and allies of the Sibling Species, and had risked all in coming to the aid of Humanity when it seemed the Faceless could not be stopped.

The T'lack of the First Iteration had exterminated Humanity.

But now she looked at that exhausted version of herself without alarm, and with a wistful smile. "You saved us, my friend. You'll never know for sure, and I can never fix that. But you saved us all, in the end. You did very well, indeed."

With that trauma at least, Alicia realized, she was at peace.

7. The Drones

At home, later that day, Alicia received a call from Jeanine.

"I just spoke with Dr. Newcomb," Jeanine said. "I understand her reluctance to move forward with the usual techniques. No argument there, given all the variables and unknowns. I've never heard of anything like this. You know, they might even name this condition after you."

Alicia laughed, delighted to hear her friend make even a grim joke. A conversation with Robert had revealed that Jeanine had understated the darkness of her own situation. "I think I could live with that, so long as it remains a little-known diagnosis."

"That's for damned sure."

"So, when do we begin?" Alicia asked.

"Unfortunately, I was quite correct that the

impending visit from my in-laws will delay the start of our sessions," Jeanine said, clearly unhappy with her situation. "Really sorry about that."

"It's not your fault," Alicia replied. "I'll be here whenever you're ready."

"We'll start as soon as they're gone."

The delay was regrettable, but Alicia had come away from her conversation with Simone knowing that, while things were more complicated than she had realized, she was not dealing with it on her own. The people who had brought her back, Simone especially, were watching over her. Knowing this relieved some of the anxiety she'd felt, and made it easier to relax into normal life as she went through the days that followed. She found it easier to laugh, especially at the antics of the children. Alicia could see in the faces of those she loved most, Robert and Melep, Vurn and Paul – Sylvia remained aloof – that the Alicia they knew was coming back to them. She was more clearly with them and sharing their moments with each passing day. Seeing this fed into her ability to accept what was real, however unsettling certain aspects of reality might be.

Whatever demons yet lurked in her mind, they were safely locked away, rendered impotent. It was not a cure, exactly, living this quiet day-to-day existence, so familiar and so dear. Alicia knew herself well enough, and was honest enough, to admit that. There remained the risk, however slight, that something might disturb the sequestration protocols. But when

Alicia investigated the Hroom alterations to those protocols, mentioned by Simone, she was both impressed and reassured by what she saw.

There was a feeling of catching one's breath.

Came the day the children ran into the house when called to lunch, shouting *"mama'licia,"* when they saw her at home for the midday meal; she normally had lunch at the SSI. All three of them called her so, including little Sylvia, who now not only accepted Alicia's embrace but returned it. She looked up from where she knelt to return the girl's hug and saw the look of relief on Melep's face, and that meant as much as the child's acceptance. It was only in that moment that Alicia realized how deeply concerned her *eli'sana* was about the matter.

That evening, Robert returned from his work in the Bartram habitat vineyards with news that something odd was taking place in the star system beyond the enormous metal and stone shell that enclosed their inverted world.

"Heard something strange today, from a coworker," he said after dinner. The children had disappeared, returning to whatever had occupied them that day. He poured *bosh'sh*, a Leyra'an liquor, into three glasses. Around the upper deck the multicolored elf lights gave a soft glow; the light was easy on the eyes. "Courier drones are appearing at the node in unusual numbers. They're following standard automatic traffic control commands, and so there's been no official reaction to the influx. But it's unusual enough that the newsfeed highlighted it."

"Does anyone know what sort of data they're bringing?" Melep asked.

He shook his head as he replied. "Not yet, but they're downloading whatever they have directly to the Library Annex, which responds to inquiries on the matter with a 'please stand by' message."

"Well, that might actually explain things," Alicia said. "If there have been major advances or changes somewhere, the data would be added to the Annex for processing before open access begins. We'll know soon enough what's being brought in."

"I thought of that, and you're probably right," he said. "But if this is some sort of massive update, it's being handled strangely. For one thing, I've never seen integration and release take this long. If it isn't proper to release it in stages as the drones come in, the Annex should say so. Instead – 'please stand by.' Another thing that makes this all so odd, in addition to the number of drones coming in, is how long they stay docked to the Annex."

"You mean linked, don't you?" Alicia asked.

"No, they're flying from the node, past Serch'nach star station and Bartram, and physically docking with the Annex before beginning a download," he told her.

"Why would they do such a thing?" Melep asked.

The very question had been at the tip of

Alicia's tongue. "They wouldn't," she said. "At least, they wouldn't need to. Unless..." She hesitated, uncomfortable with the thought that had occurred to her.

"Unless?" Robert prompted.

"Unless there's a security issue involved." The words felt foreign as she spoke them. Data security was a thing unfamiliar in the openness of the Human Commonwealth, where all data was held as the common property of everyone, Human and Artificial alike. They had only become familiar with the concept of data security during the Faceless War, and now the political upheaval in what was left of the Human Republic had kept the practice in place. To say it was now familiar in no way meant Commonwealth members of the Grand Concordance were at all comfortable with the notion of concealment when it came to information.

"Security?" Robert's eyebrows rose as he repeated the word.

"The best message system we have can still be intercepted during transmission, even if it isn't an open broadcast," Alicia replied. "And any encryption can be broken, eventually. But if you directly feed the data in through a physical port with an Artificial in control of the process, the possibility of data being leaked becomes as close to zero as I can imagine."

"It begs a question, as you Humans would put it," Melep said. "Why would the Annex be receiving such sensitive data, and so frequently?" Her frown puckered the scales on her forehead. “Where are these drones coming from?”

“Probeships,” Robert told her.

“Probeships?” Alicia echoed. “The data is being withheld, but not the identities of the senders?”

“Standard traffic control,” Robert said. “They can’t enter the system without broadcasting an identification code. Anyone listening can pick it up, so that data is in the newsfeed.”

“Which ships?” Alicia asked.

“More than I can reel off by name in one sitting,” he said. “According to the newsfeed, probeships from about one percent of the Commonwealth Survey’s fleet have sent drones here.”

“How many ships are in the fleet?” Melep asked.

“One hundred and fifty thousand was the last count I have in my memory hoard,” Robert replied.

“We’ve had fifteen hundred drones through here?” Alicia asked, unable to conceal her disbelief.

“In a little over a month,” Robert said. “I haven’t been paying proper attention to the newsfeed since you came home. And there's a harvest to manage. Someone mentioned the matter while we were harvesting grapes this morning, or I’d still be in the dark.”

“And I’ve been too distracted with catch-up work to bother with news at all,” Alicia admitted.

On that matter, Melep was silent. They all knew she was the very opposite of a news addict.

"It's strange," Robert said with a shrug. He poured himself another serving of bright red *bosh'sh*, replenishing the other two glasses when they were held out to him. "But so far no alarms have been raised, so there's no crisis involved. Just a lot of data dumps from a large number of Artificials. Sooner or later, it'll all come out, I'm sure."

The idea of out-waiting a mystery being contrary to her nature, Alicia said, "I'm going to make some inquires on the matter."

"Others have tried," Melep pointed out. "They were told to 'stand by.'"

"So far," Robert said. "According to the newsfeed, at least."

"Can't hurt to try," Alicia said, sipping the drink. She felt the heat of its considerable alcohol content, knowing the nanomed would prevent her from getting anything but a mild buzz. Years before, on her first exposure to the beverage, the detox setting had been too low for the fortified beverage beloved by the Leyra'an. The experience had left her with some embarrassment to live down.

"Let us know if you learn anything," Melep said.

"Of course."

That very evening, Alicia entered a request for information on the matter of message drones from the Commonwealth. She used her ID as director of the Sibling Species Institute to send the inquiry through official channels. The response she received from the Library Annex, an Artificial that curated the flow of information into the star system, was immediate and short.

"Your request is being processed. Please stand by."

8. What Dreams May Come

That night, as the three of them slept, only two knew the peace of dreamless slumber.

Alicia dozed off in a large, warm, cozy bed, tucked in with her husband and *eli'sana*. She woke abruptly in a place cold and dark. It was nothing at all like her previous awakening, from her induced coma. Then she had been acutely aware of nothingness. Now she was just as sharply aware that she was inside something, an unyielding cylinder that blocked all light and sound. She pressed up with her palms, and panic surged as the sense of entrapment overwhelmed her. Alicia shouted, but heard only the flat reflection of her own voice, without answer.

What is this? Where the hell am I? How

did I get here?

This didn't feel like any dream she could recall, and Alicia had experienced some lucid dreams in her life. This was real. She could feel the cold, unyielding barrier that held her inside whatever this space was called. But that was impossible. And then, just as impossible, she was outside that close confinement, falling, tumbling head over heels through the cold and the dark. She struck something, caught at it, then tumbled away, tearing loose a handful of something brown that crumbled away between her fingers. It took a moment to realize she held a fistful of dead, dry tree leaves.

She was in the dark, frozen corpse of the lost *William Bartram*. Somehow, she just knew this.

Impossible! The ship is gone! The Willie B doesn't exist anymore!

The lost probeship had been dismantled and rendered down to provide some of the building materials for its namesake habitat. Every scrap had been recycled, including the biomass of dead animals and plants, the soil, the air, and the water. Nothing remained.

A dream. A nightmare, no matter how real it feels. It has to be.

And yet it was as real and tangible as the dinner her family had shared that evening. With this realization came another, that she was naked in the blackness and vacuum filling the dead ship. She could not breathe.

Another abrupt change, this time a sense of up and down and of truly falling. Alicia twisted to get her feet under her. She would have released the fistful of leaves to have both hands free, but the abrupt nonexistence of those leaves left her shaking out an already empty hand. She was falling toward light. Into light.

Alicia was encased in combat armor and alarms were blaring. Around her were jumbled, unrecognizable ruins. She stood alone; scattered around her were bodies, bent and broken. As she watched, the bodies rose with awkward jerks of limbs and necks, then turned toward her with sightless eyes that blazed with silver light. Backing away from this horrific sight, she checked her weapons and power, and found the first at zero and the latter badly depleted, falling toward zero even as she found the readout. She would be utterly helpless before the rising horde of Faceless victims, all of them with silver light now bursting through open wounds.

Robert shifted in his sleep and put an arm around her. Alicia almost shouted in shock and surprise, but bit back on the outcry, unwilling to awaken her partners. She was in their bed, Robert with his face against her shoulder, Melep on the other side, snoring softly. The vague not quite darkness of the habitat filled their room, open as it was on one wall. She was warm and safe and with those she loved most in all the universe. And she was covered with a cold sweat when she realized this was every bit as real as all the rest she had just experienced.

At least, it seemed that way.

In the nightmare there had been no sound.

An unnatural silence had filled the experience. Sight and touch had been her only senses. Now she could hear Robert breathing and Melep quietly snoring. She took a deep breath and sighed. So it had been a bad dream after all, creepy and horribly real as it had seemed. And felt.

She put her hand on Robert's arm and felt the warmth of it, the solidity. In a few minutes the nanomed reregulated her system, removing the adrenaline the nightmare had generated, and in a little more time she finally slept. This time with no dreams.

9. Memory Hoard

Alicia didn't immediately tell Robert and Melep about the disturbance to her sleep. It wasn't that the dream faded in the light of day, drifting into that obscure realm of not-quite-memory as dreams usually do. The nightmare she had endured the previous night did nothing of the sort. Upon awakening, she remembered it all too clearly, as if the images were memories from the events of the previous day. Not at all sure what to say, and having no desire to worry her partners, she left well enough alone for the moment. This was a matter to discuss first with Simone and Jeanine; she was not inclined to burden her family with something that would upset them, possibly for no real reason. So she indulged in the usual morning chatter with partners and children, preparing for her day and helping the others prepare for theirs.

A call to Jeanine brought up an apologetic

recording that the family matter still had her tied up. Alicia left a message, requesting a response as soon as possible, saying only that she'd had a puzzling experience and thought Jeanine should know about it.

Message sent, she traveled by tram to the SSI, as always enjoying the feeling of being in the open, passing clusters of residences and fields of varying crops of vegetables, herbs, and flowers. Strange as her night had been, this particular morning felt fresh and bright and beautiful, and the unease with which she had awakened faded – even if the dream images lingered. And so she was in a decent enough mood that survived even the melancholy sight of the war memorial at the front gates. She paused to look upon the holographic likenesses of her lost friends, and sighed. Whatever mood she might ever be in, Alicia was resolved that, upon passing this place, she would never fail to pause and pay her respects.

Midday came, still without word from Jeanine. Desiring company for the noon meal, she checked Tuleselan's office to invite him to join her, but he wasn't there. Hoping for some spontaneous companionship, Alicia went down to the ground floor, and into the spacious cafeteria. It was open to the park along one wall; bird song drifted over the murmur of multiple conversations. And there she found Simone Newcomb just joining the line.

"Hello, Simone," she said. "Would you mind some company?"

"Not at all. Please, join me."

They worked their way along the counter, making selections, then picked a table with two chairs just outside of the cafeteria proper. As they sat down, Simone asked, "Have you and Dr. Milhouse been able to make a start?"

"Not yet," Alicia replied. "She's caught up in some sort of family matter."

"Nothing serious, I hope."

Alicia shook her head a little. "Well, that remains to be seen. A visit from her in-laws, from the Republic. She didn't say much, but I got the impression these relatives are trying to get the Milhouses to *return* to the Republic."

"I saw something on the newsfeed recently," Simone said. "President Worth's government is trying to call former citizens back, to help with rebuilding and reconsolidating the Republic. It didn't sound like he was getting the response he hoped for."

"He won't get it from the Milhouses," Alicia asserted. "Or if they do decide to go back, they'll be leaving their daughter Rebecca behind. She's made it plain that Bartram Habitat is home. Period."

"Sounds like a determined person," Simone said. "How old is she?"

"Thirteen – no, she'd be fifteen now. And she was a force to be reckoned with when she was just entering her teens. Refused to be evacuated with the other children."

"Like her older sister," Simone observed.

"Not quite," Alicia said. "Becca was a noncombatant, but she was standing her ground with her family, no matter how unstable that orbit turned out to be. At any rate, from what my partners are telling me, the Milhouses are firmly settled here, and are official citizens of the Concordance. Or, no, it's the Grand Concordance now."

"A good name for it," Simone said, glancing around. The room was dominated by Humans, but the multispecies population of the habitat, and the SSI in particular, was on full display. A table near theirs was surrounded by Grahlin having an animated discussion. Not far off a Nesvama and two Leyra'an women were sharing a quiet meal. At an outsized table and bench sat a Hroom, facing a T'lack, who was perched on one of the odd metal stools they used instead of chairs. The Hroom was consuming what appeared to be a mountain of scrambled eggs. T'lack did not feed in public, the fulfillment of their dietary needs being a disturbing sight to most people. "This was all just stories and pictures until I was summoned here to help with cases like yours. Seeing it for real, living among all these other beings – it's just amazing."

"I grew up convinced nothing of the sort would ever be seen," Alicia said. "Likely you did as well." To which Simone merely nodded agreement. "Now, I can't imagine it being any other way."

"I wouldn't *want* it any other way."

Alicia worked at her salad for a moment. "You said 'cases like yours.' And earlier, you said a few others had come out of their comas."

"Seven so far, counting you," Simone

replied. She took a sip of her coffee, then added, "Survivors who were in various vital or emergency services. They were outside the shelters, but wore powered armor suits similar to yours to aid them in their work during the crisis. Their shielding was comparable to the military-grade electromag armor around the suit you wore. It responded to the pulse by, as far as we've been able to determine, canceling it out for all but a mere split second. As brief as the effect was, it was apparently enough to cause massive damage to your central nervous system. Unlike your situation, none of the other six had auxiliary memory hoards, so whatever feedback happened to damage the hoards, they are currently without the use of such devices. We still don't understand why you still have access to your standard issue. Just one more mystery on a growing list."

"But they otherwise have the same situation?"

Simone nodded. "They all woke up screaming, reliving what was happening to them when the device detonated. Like you, all of them were in immediate danger of being assimilated by the Faceless hordes when the Pulsar went off. Unlike you, memory sequestration wasn't an option for any of them. No functional memory hoards. So the necessary patterns were recorded and then erased from their organic memories."

"Rob told me there were a lot of people hurt when the Pulsar device went off," Alicia said. "People who weren't so well protected.

How have things gone for them?"

"Most of them died that day," Simone replied, looking down into her coffee mug. "Some were revived, but with their memories either scrambled or not there at all." She grimaced and added, "The worst off are those who entered catatonic states."

"Catatonia?"

"Apparently irreversible." Simone ate a few bites of her sandwich, appetite apparently unimpaired by the subject under discussion. "There's not a lot more we can do for those, except provide support care. The nanomedical technology we have, which now incorporates innovations from the other Sibling Species, can only repair the neurological damage. It can restore the synaptic connections, but can't rewrite memories. It can't recreate minds. Many of those who are not catatonic are starting all over again as adult-sized children."

They sat for a moment, each studying the remaining contents of her coffee mug. Finally, Alicia asked, "Do any of the other six like me report strange dreams?"

Simone stopped eating and stared at Alicia, startled. "Strange?" she asked. "What do you mean by strange?"

To the best of her ability, which was all too good considering how clear her memories of the previous night were, Alicia described what she had experienced. The look on Simone's face grew into a frown as Alicia spoke, but she never interrupted. When she finished her account, Alicia said, "I get the feeling from the way you're looking at me that this is either not a surprise, or bad news."

"It's not, and it is, I'm afraid," Simone replied. "No one else has reported lucid dreams, yet, but what you're describing sounds familiar."

"So, it's not the result of what the Pulsar device did to me?"

"Maybe not directly," Simone said. "At least, that's my guess right now, and assuming this is the symptom I'm familiar with."

"Symptom of what? Gaia, just what I need, a new malady!"

"Oh, if it's what I think it is, it's nothing we can't take care of," Simone assured her hastily. "But, yes, I've seen something like this before. What you're describing may be a memory hoard malfunction."

"There's no longer anything to do with the probeship disaster in my hoard," Alicia said.

"So the Bartram disaster memories are no longer sequestered?"

"No, they're simply a part of my organic memory collection," Alicia replied.

"One of the functions of a hoard is to allow realistic recall of selected stored personal experiences," Simone explained.

"I know."

"What I think may be happening is that the realistic recall functionality is intruding on normal brain activity," Simone said. "It's taking an existing memory — in this case your experience aboard the wrecked *William Bartram* — and reinforcing it as if it's a memory hoard file, which it is *not* supposed to do. That's what made those images seem so real, and most likely explains why they feel like recent memories now."

"It did better than make it all *seem* real," Alicia said. "Hell, it did *much* worse than that. And what about the other sequences?"

"They all at least draw from fragments in your organic memory," Simone pointed out. "You can't remember those last few minutes of the war, but you do know about the Faceless terror weapon and how it worked. So there was something to draw on for that sequence. This syndrome happens during REM sleep, amplifying random bits of memory, along with whatever imaginative processes are involved with dreaming."

"How did I end up in this situation?" Alicia asked. "Is it related to the physical damage I endured?"

"Almost certainly," Simone said. "I'm familiar with the symptoms because this is not an uncommon side effect of other forms of neurological trauma."

"You said we can take care of this?" Alicia gave what was left of her lunch a last poke with the fork, and then abandoned it.

"First, I'll run a diagnostic of your functional hoard to be sure that what I described is the cause," Simone replied. "I need to see what sort of fault indicators, if any, show up. That data will tell me exactly how to proceed. This will all take a few days."

"More to the point, a few nights," Alicia

said, trying not to groan aloud. There was a bleak, angry feeling rising in her. "Meaning it could happen again."

"If I'm right about this, it probably *will* happen again," Simone replied. "Sorry about that."

The comm system announced itself with a single bell tone and Simone's name. "Accept all," she said, and a dataframe opened over the table between them. The side facing Alicia was pale blue but featureless, indicating the message was a private one for Simone. She couldn't see Simone through it, but what she heard was as alarming as it was revealing.

"Three of them?" Simone asked. Alicia couldn't hear the other voice. "I would expect so. I'm sitting here with Alicia, and she's just given me a similar story. Yes, rather upset about it. I want you to contact the rest, see what's going on with them. And see if they can all manage to meet us at the Institute this afternoon. Thanks, Sharon." The dataframe vanished.

"I'm almost afraid to ask..."

"If you've guessed that you're no longer the only one with realistic dreams, bad ones, you've got it right." Simone frowned, shaking her head a little. "This doesn't make sense. What you describe fits the diagnostic criteria for a memory hoard malfunction, but of the seven who've awakened, you're the only one with a functioning memory hoard." She sat for a long moment, staring into space, clearly lost in thought.

"Simone?"

"I'm at a loss," Simone admitted, looking up and meeting Alicia's eyes. "This clearly can't be the syndrome I described to you."

"The timing," said Alicia.

"It's one hell of a coincidence," Simone replied.

"If it *is* a coincidence," Alicia said.

"Well, you were all brought out of your comas within a few hours of each other," said Simone. "If we accidentally set this in motion, somehow, it would make sense that symptoms would develop within a narrow window of time."

"I suppose so," Alicia said quietly. She suddenly had the feeling she'd missed something, but couldn't put her finger on what felt wrong.

"We need data," Simone said. "So far all we have is a set of anecdotes."

"Familiar territory, for me," Alicia said. "Brand new problem, and we need data before any conclusions can be drawn. The question then becomes, how do we get the data we need?"

Simone was nodding as Alicia spoke, and when she was finished, Simone said, "Right now, I'm using nanomed telemetry to monitor your physical health, but it's only giving me basic neurological data. That's all the system is set up to handle. So we need to refine the orbit, focus on specifics."

"What parameters do you have in mind?"

Another comm alert came before Simone

could answer. “What’s the word, Sharon?”

This time, Alicia could hear both sides of the conversation. “I’ve been in touch with the other three, and it’s happened to all of them.”

“Do we have a sense for times of occurrence?” Simone asked.

“Not really,” Sharon replied. “Just that it was last night.”

“I was afraid of that,” Simone muttered.

“I’ve scheduled a meeting later this afternoon.” Sharon specified the hour. “Everyone is willing to attend in person.”

“Perfect,” said Simone. “I want to set everyone up with neural monitors keyed to REM function and memory activation, with twenty-four-hour continuous download. I want to be able to monitor what’s happening in real-time. You know the drill.”

“Consider it done,” said Sharon. The dataframe blinked out.

“If you haven't already done so, tell your partners about these nightmares,” Simone said. “I believe they need to know this is going on.”

“I’ll tell them tonight,” Alicia assured her. With a short, nervous laugh, she added, “Well, this is certainly a new one for me.”

“What do you mean?” Simone raised her mug and took a healthy drink of coffee.

“I’ve spent my entire adult life gathering and analyzing data points. Now I’m about to become one.” She laughed again, and felt just a little of her tension ease as a result. “So, does that make me a collaborator, or a subject?”

Simone saluted her with the mug. “It

makes you my patient." She set the mug down and stood up. "I need to get back to work. In the meantime, try not to worry."

"Who's worried?" Alicia asked with mild sarcasm.

"Anyone with a gram of sense."

10. Others

The impromptu appointment was late enough in the afternoon that Alicia decided against using it as an excuse to cancel her meetings with new staff members. She held a few of these every other day, after lunch, as part of her efforts to get back into the routine of the Institute; this happened to be one of those days, and was the next to last one she would need for the purpose. Alicia didn't regret the effort – it was certainly necessary to know these new people – but it took an emotional toll. Each new face reminded her of one gone beyond recall.

There was no help for it. She could endure the necessity or step down, and after all that had been done on her behalf to make the situation as tolerable as possible, giving up was not an option Alicia even briefly entertained.

So she met the new faces, welcoming them as they offered welcome to her. Very early in this process of meet-and-greet, Alicia realized all of them had a common aspect of behavior. Their deference to her went beyond respect for the position she had resumed. It was closer to awe – or hero worship – and both the Leyra'an and Nesvama staffers were especially obvious, with their bows and formal phrases. This day was no different from the rest, in that regard.

Hero.

Alicia scoffed silently at the notion, even as she realized that, from their perspective, she was exactly that. She completely understood why Robert felt as he did about his status as a war hero. It was not a comfortable feeling, and would never be something she found acceptable. Alicia could only hope that these new staffers would, in time, become sufficiently familiar with who and what she really was that the awe in which they all held her would fade.

As her last visitors, a pair of Grahlin clone sisters, left her office, a message came from Simone. They were ready ahead of schedule, and she could come in for the monitor implants at any time. Lacking a reason to delay until the appointed hour, which was all of thirty minutes away in any case, Alicia took the lift down to that level and made her way to Simone's clinic. Half a dozen people, all Human, were there already, and Simone's assistant Sharon, clad in medtech blue, was going from one to the next, taking med data from their internal nanomed systems using a small handheld device that was almost hidden between her fingers.

"Hello, Sharon," Alicia said as she sat down.

Sharon smiled, held the shiny blue and black device toward her, and took the download she needed. "You know, I'm rather flattered that you remember me. We never actually worked together."

"But you were always here, so you're a familiar face," Alicia said. "That makes you stand out, these days. For me, at any rate."

"Believe me, I know just what you mean," Sharon said. Quite abruptly, she lowered her gaze, her face half-hidden by loose brown hair. She made no effort to meet Alicia's eyes. "I was – elsewhere when things blew up. I was *supposed* to be here, but I traded shifts with..." She stopped speaking abruptly.

Someone who died instead. The thought was there, but left unspoken. Looking past the medtech, Alicia saw the concern on Simone's face. She put her hand on Sharon's shoulder and said, "I know how you feel," quietly enough to avoid being overheard. "Why am I still here, when so many others weren't so fortunate? It's hard to take."

"You feel that sort of guilt?" Sharon asked, looking up at her, dark eyes glittering with tears.

"Every day since I came to," Alicia assured her. "You have people here, still?"

"Yes," Sharon replied. "My family. They evacuated to Eriola. Came home when it was safe."

"My husband was out there in the thick of things," Alicia said. "My *ara'sana* was here, with me, in the fight. Everyone else was at Eriola. Holm was killed, but I'm still here." She sighed and let go of Sharon's shoulder. "There's no rhyme or reason to why we're alive and others are not. It just happened that way. You couldn't have known the Faceless was coming here. No one expected it. Feeling guilt or remorse is understandable, of course it is. Best way to deal with it, I've found, is to hang on to that family. Lean on them as much as they'll let you."

"They do what they can," said Sharon with a barely visible nod.

"Mine, too."

"I'm in a support group," Sharon said. "We, ah, talk about these things — it helps. Would you be interested in joining?"

"I would indeed," Alicia replied. "I'll soon be working with a friend who is trained to deal with a situation like this, but I also meant to seek out a group like yours."

"I'll send you the next meeting time and place." Smiling again, Sharon turned toward Simone and said, "We're updated. No problems detected."

"Great," Simone said. "Let's get this done, then."

What needed to be done was a simple enough matter. The monitors that would track the brain function of Alicia and her fellow patients were microscopic devices, similar in structure to the micro-machines of the nanomed system itself. They would become part of that system, in fact. They were inserted in pairs, one of which would find its way to the hippocampus, while its counterpart migrated to the visual cortex. Insertion required the same touch of an adhesive patch used to administer nanomed, so no one so much as fluttered an eyelid in discomfort.

The patients seeking Simone's help, all of them members of the support group Sharon had mentioned, introduced themselves and chatted for a few minutes as they relaxed and waited for confirmation that the monitors were in place and fully functional. All of them being survivors of the Pulsar device detonation that had disabled the enemy, a sense of camaraderie developed quickly. Like Alicia, each held a locked-up memory hoard that acted as if it were at full capacity. What set Alicia apart was the fact that it was her auxiliary hoard that was damaged.

"Best guess," said Simone, when it was asked how such a thing could happen, "is that the size of the data load triggered a standard memory hoard protocol, shunting the influx to the auxiliary structure."

"You're almost certainly right," said Alicia. "The system is designed to bring the aux hoard online if the rate of data flow goes above a certain level. That's to keep the standard hoard free for daily use. Now, why there was no damage to the standard hoard when the aux hit capacity..." And she shrugged.

"Another guess," said Simone, "is that the

Pulsar device disrupted whatever was happening, preventing continued download."

"In other words," said Alicia, "I got lucky."

"It happens," said Simone.

"And all of that in a microsecond," Sharon added.

"Time is relative," said Alicia.

"Frankly, I'm more interested in the fix than the cause," said a man named Alejandro. "I mean, we all have backups elsewhere, but we can't access those until our systems have been cleaned up."

"I'm puzzled that our blocked-up hoards can still mess with our dreams," said one named Burt. "I mean, I can see that happening to Alicia, but..."

"It implies that the hoards are not actually ruined, just dysfunctional," said Simone. "I don't know that for a fact, but it's plausible. That's why we're using these monitors. I need to look very closely at the data as we gather it, real time, before we form any conclusions. What I suspect is that some of the basic programming may be intact and still integrated to some degree with your normal brain functions. That could be the source of these nocturnal disturbances. If this surmise turns out to be correct, we're a step closer to a solution."

When things had been checked and double-checked, and all was in order, they went their separate ways, Alicia with a "See you later, then" to Sharon as they parted company.

Back at her office, Alicia found that Jeanine

had at last returned her call, and was able to call back and make contact. As soon as they faced each other, in the holographic sense, Alicia filled her friend in on recent events. The recounting left Jeanine frowning and shaking her head. "Something about all this makes me uncomfortable," she said.

"Which part, the support group?" Alicia asked, realizing only then that seeking out such a group might imply lack of confidence in Jeanine's skills.

"Oh, no, not that." Jeanine gave a dismissive wave of her hand. "That's actually a fine idea, one I should have suggested. No, I'm worrying about the idea that your memory hoard is casting about for memories to feed into the dream state. What if it breaks the sequestration protocols in the process?"

"Damn, I should have thought of that," Alicia admitted. "We need to pass that worry along to Simone."

"We need to get in there and deal with what you experienced the day Holm was killed," Jeanine told her. "That way, if it malfunctions, you'll already have some control over the situation."

"That's pretty much what Simone is aiming at, after all," Alicia said. "But we need to understand how this interaction is occurring, and why."

"I'm not arguing against that, not at all," Jeanine assured her. "What worries me is the damage that could be done if this – malfunction, or whatever it is, grabs the traumatic memory before we have some foundation in place for dealing with it." She paused, as if thinking something through, then said, "The part of the dream in the probeship – you managed that well enough?"

"I suppose so," Alicia replied. "It was alarming, but once I recognized it for what it was, I could control my reactions. Well, more or less."

"That's a result of the work we did on it, together," Jeanine told her, nodding and looking relieved. "And that's actually very good news. Those control techniques aren't specific to the old memories. You aren't exactly defenseless if something slips."

"That's good to know."

"I understand Dr. Newcomb's desire to move cautiously," Jeanine went on to say. "But with this latest development, I think we need to balance caution with getting things done, and move forward with the therapy. The sooner that experience becomes just a bad memory, and not a demon haunting your inner life, the better."

Alicia frowned, surprised to hear the matter expressed in such dramatic terms, and with such urgency. "I'll relay all of this to Simone."

"I see she's left a message while I was tied up," Jeanine said. "I'll contact her when we're done with the family visit over here."

"Having your own problems, still?" Alicia asked, noting that her friend sounded tired.

"Yes." Jeanine closed her eyes and slowly

shook her head. "But not for much longer, I'm happy to report. Greg's folks are getting ready to leave. His brother and sister-in-law returned to Webster System yesterday, on their way back into the Republic proper to hire a law firm. The fact that the Republic isn't a part of the Grand Concordance, and has no legal jurisdiction here, doesn't register with them."

"What do they hope to accomplish?"

"They want custody of Rebecca."

"And they think they'll get it how? By suing you? Or the GC?"

Jeanine shrugged and said, "They've gone stark raving, 'Licia. There's nothing of reason left to them. Anyway, his parents will be here for another day or two, at most. Greg is trying to treat them well, but they are – unpleasant."

"In what way?"

"If they fail in their effort to 'rescue' Becca – their word for it – his father will seek to formally disown him. By the laws of the Republic, I mean."

"People actually do such things over there?" Alicia asked. "For the Leyra'an, that would be unthinkable. For the Rusalas, from what I'm told, it would be a matter of life and death."

"Afraid so, although it isn't common." The frown that was settling in shifted to a look of defiance. "My husband was not so easily antagonized. He told them that, if that's how things are to be, we have all the family we could need, right here. Also pointed out that the laws of the Republic are legally null in the Grand

Concordance."

"I'm tempted to say good for him, but..."

"Yes," Jeanine said, nodding. "Not as easily endured as declared."

"You know he's right, of course," Alicia said. "About having family here."

Defiance was replaced by a little smile. "Yes, we know. And that makes the difference. A big part of why we *won't* go back. You people have always been there for us, like a true family."

"I hope someday Greg's family is as understanding as yours turned out to be," Alicia said.

"I honestly don't see that happening," Jeanine said with a short, humorless laugh. "By the way, my folks and my younger brother just relocated to Webster System shortly after it seceded from the Republic and joined the GC. I can't wait for them to come here for a visit, so we can show them the life we have here in Bartram. I want to introduce them to all of you. And speaking of all of you, when do we gather at the Willow Lake Inn?"

"Tomorrow evening," Alicia replied.

"Good," Jeanine said with an assertive nod. "Greg could use some cheering up after all of this. My god, that father of his." She rolled her eyes. "He tried to use Becca to manipulate us."

"Use her? How?"

"Made a point of telling her that, because of her parents' attitudes, she would never see him again."

"Oh, Mother of Life," Alicia said, closing

her eyes for a moment. "That poor girl." To her surprise, the response from her friend began with a snort of rude laughter.

"Poor girl my ass," Jeanine said. "She looked that old man straight in the eye and said, 'Your loss.'"

"She didn't!"

"Oh, she certainly did." Jeanine was grinning hugely. "I was so proud of her."

They both had a laugh at that, although Jeanine's laugh had a bitter edge, and then Alicia said, "You know, I really need to get back to work."

"I'll contact Simone right away," Jeanine replied. "Be well, my friend."

When her friend's image blinked out, Alicia organized some files for the next day's effort and left the SSI, homeward bound. She shared the tram ride with strangers who recognized her from newsfeed exposure and chatted amiably about nothing of consequence. Walking through her front door a short time later, she was quickly swept up by family, augmented by the Nol'ez family, who lived not far away. Nol'ez was the Leyra'an version of Knowles; John Knowles and his partner Wirolen were old friends, and their daughter Jaxi was a favored playmate of the Rost'aht-MacGregor children. The quartet of offspring swarmed her, laughing and chattering, a hopeless babble of voices that Alicia made no attempt to sort out; she just let it wash over her. There was a definite therapeutic effect from the noise and energy.

Six-year-old Jaxi always caught her eye. Bright and precocious, with a boldness that reminded Alicia of the girl's great-grandmother, the justly famous Eb'shra Maladar. The physical resemblance that might have gone with that of personality was muted by the fact that Jaxi was half Human. She was the first ever fusion child, a hybrid of Human and Leyra'an genetic material, using techniques devised by the Hroom. Her eyes were Human blue, like her father's, but Leyra'an hair – black like her mother's – surrounded her head like a mane. Jaxi was fond of the full effect of her hair, unlike Wirolen, who kept hers cut very short. Leyra'an scales of a cinnamon brown hue covered the upper surface of her arms, her shoulders, and her cheeks. A pretty girl, Alicia had no doubt she would one day be noted as a great beauty, like her mother and great-grandmother, albeit for somewhat different reasons.

In a flash, their greeting was done, and Alicia stood in the palpable energy wake of youngsters racing off to play, a warbling han'anga in hot pursuit.

Home, indeed.

Before they began preparing the evening meal, Alicia called a conference, including the Nol'ez adults, whose insights had so often been valuable in the past. She told them all of the bizarre waking dream, Simone's take on the matter, and Jeanine's concerns. Almost in passing, she mentioned the monitors and the support group involving Simone's assistant,

Sharon. The current approach to the situation was discussed, and it was agreed that it was sensible.

"I find it reassuring that both Simone and Jeanine are helping you with this," said Melep.

"If they work together as well as Simone did with Tuleselan, you'll be in good hands," said Robert.

"I'm certainly finding Simone easy to work with," Alicia said. "There's something about her that feels, I don't know – comfortable. Familiar." She shrugged, unsure of what words would adequately express her feelings.

"She's one of those people who just naturally falls into your orbit," Robert said, nodding in agreement. "We both felt that way, when we met her."

"*Yia*," Melep said, her Leyra'an word for agreement carrying more force in Alicia's hearing than the translator's rendering. "That is how it was. As if she was supposed to be there with us, all along. *A'a'jalot.*" Meaning a thing meant to be.

"I feel left out," said Wirolen. "I must meet this woman someday."

"She'll join us at the Willow Lake Inn for the party, tomorrow night," said Alicia. "I'll be sure to introduce you."

With that, a good dinner with friends, and the comforting presence of the two she loved most in the universe, Alicia called it a night. The bed was warm and snug, and she relaxed into what she dearly hoped would be a good night's sleep.

11. Lucidity

She drowsed, then was aware that she was no longer warm and snug. She was in an EVA suit, drifting in the dark, a dead brown tree passing slowly below her feet. Terror welled up, swiftly tamped down by surging awareness that she'd already been through this. She was reliving the day she had tried to lead the initial salvage operations aboard the wrecked *William Bartram* – in the very moment panic had overwhelmed her. With this awareness, she used the tricks Jeanine had taught her, brief meditations that controled her breathing and steadied her heart rate, even as she continued to dream of floating through that dead, dark place.

How am I able to do this?

Refusing to re-enact the event, even in a dream, Alicia fully expected the dream-state to be overridden by her conscious intentions. It didn't happen that way. Alicia felt the suit around her, smelled it, and heard faint radio traffic. She manipulated the jet controls to do a slow spin, looking for the others of her team. Suited figures, their EVA gear brightly lit, were all around her. It was all as real as the crowd of noisy friends and family around the dinner table had been. She was, as far as she could tell, wide awake, which was impossible. Even as she thought this, and completed the turn toward her teammates, Alicia realized the helmeted figures were filling with silver light, shining through faceplates, then through every joint and seal of the EVA suits they wore.

Faceless! As she recognized the light, the suited forms became nothing but silvery bright humanoid shapes. The remains of the fallen, taken by the enemy.

There was a clear flight line back to the main hatch through which the team had entered. Heart pounding, Alicia fired the suit's jets and flew headlong back the way she'd come. She knew full well that these apparitions were just that, but the sight of the Faceless automatons was more than she could bear, waking dream or not. And so she fled the scene.

And the scene changed. Alicia was watching the door of a lift tube slide open, her heart still hammering in her chest. Excited people stood around her: great, hulking Hroom, dwarfish Grahlin, Leyra'an wearing tri-colored sashes called *es'avas*, ebony Nesvama in colorful robes, and Humans. They were about to welcome the T'lack aboard the Bartram habitat. The T'lack of the First Iteration had exterminated Humanity, and yet, in this timeline, were allies of the Sibling Species. Alicia was determined to give the insectoid beings all the benefit of the proverbial doubt, the T'lack of this Iteration being very different creatures. The door was open and three T'lack emerged, gaunt and angular, their movements stiff and awkward to Human eyes. Frightful-looking beings, but all the same, Alicia stepped forward and raised an arm in greeting. A T'lack reached out and took the offered hand.

It blazed with silver light as it ripped her arm from the socket.

Screaming denials, she sat bolt upright in the bed. Robert had his arms around her and Melep was crouched on the mattress, wide-eyed, fearful. Her husband kept saying her name, telling her it was just a dream. Only a bad dream.

"Yes," she whispered, clutching at him, then freeing an arm to reach for Melep and draw her close. She huddled between them, drenched in cold sweat, shaking violently. She felt Robert tighten his grip on her, as if trying to damp down the tremors that shook her. "Yes, a bad dream. Just a bad dream."

But in her gut doubt planted a seed, nurtured by what Simone had revealed earlier that day. There was something more going on, something worse. It had been *real*. The pain had been real; her shoulder throbbed with pain, so much that she checked to make sure her arm was still attached. Even as she did so, the comm system chimed with a message coded yellow for urgency. The sender was Simone Newcomb.

"Accept, voice only," said Melep when her partners hesitated.

"Alicia?" Simone's voice came to them as if out of thin air.

"Simone, what's going on?" Robert demanded.

"Still trying to figure that out," Simone replied. "Alicia's monitor went into the red zone just a moment ago. And Sharon is talking to one of her fellow patients right now who did the same thing. Another nightmare?"

Alicia nodded, then remembered Simone couldn't see her. She had to work a moment to make words come. "Worse than the one last night. Gaia, Simone, a T'lack killed me in this one. It had been taken by the Faceless."

"Sharon just let me know that the other patient who woke from a nightmare just now is also reporting a violent confrontation." She made no mention of who she meant, or specifically what the nightmare involved. "She was apparently surprised to find she had survived, it was so realistic."

"Same here," Alicia said. "Hell, it *was* real, Simone, for all that I could tell. Sight, and this time also sound and smell. I was in the Bartram again, and knew I was dreaming. But that didn't make any difference. And I felt *pain*. I felt it when the T'lack ripped my arm off.

There was no way to convince myself it wasn't really happening." She stopped, unable to say more, trying not to burst into tears.

Melep sat back with a look of horror; whispered Leyra'an curses escaped her usual self-control, too softly uttered for the translation system to pick up. There was no need for translation. Alicia was fluent in the language of her adoptive people, and agreed completely with Melep's pungent choices.

"Same report – hold on. We have the other monitor participants checking in, all of them. None of them went red zone the way you did, but they're all badly frightened."

"More violent encounters?" Alicia guessed.

"Yes," Simone replied. "In every case."

"Simone, why are these dreams so similar?" Melep asked.

"They certainly share a common element," Simone agreed. "In itself, that isn't too surprising. All of you were actively involved in the defense of Bartram, and were injured in the same way when the Pulsar device detonated, under violent circumstances."

"I'm more interested in the similarity in timing," said Alicia. She could feel her analytical nature quickly rising and overcoming her distress. She had been presented a puzzle, and solving such was the essence of her nature.

"It must mean something," said Robert. "I mean, they all have these dreams at the same time."

"Not exactly the same times," Simone said. "But damned close, all the same. I'm still of the opinion this is a malfunction set in motion when we brought the seven of you out of your comas."

"We weren't all revived at the same time, were we?" Alicia asked.

"Ah, no, as a matter of fact..." Simone's voice trailed away, then she said, "Good call, my friend. There is a strong correlation between the time spread of awakening and the time each of you had your nightmares."

"So perhaps it really is the malfunction you suspect," said Alicia.

"Perhaps," said Simone. "One night's data is hardly enough for a firm conclusion."

"Another night like this, and I might not be capable of firm conclusions," Alicia muttered. She was suddenly exhausted, and leaned on Robert.

"I know, sorry," said Simone. "But..."

"We need more data," Alicia agreed.

"Well, the readings from the monitors show that everything has settled back to baseline," said Simone. "Including your physical readouts. And the same is happening for the others."

"Good," said Melep.

"I'll be fine, now," Alicia said. "Go see to the others if they need you and – thanks for checking up on me, Simone."

"Thanks, indeed," said Melep. "Your concern is greatly appreciated."

"Most welcome, my friends," Simone replied. "When I have a chance to parse the little data we now have, I'll send you the results. Good night, all."

"Good night, Simone," said Robert.

They sat huddled together in the near darkness, saying nothing for several minutes, then settled back down and pulled the blankets up over themselves. Robert faced Alicia, and Melep snuggled in behind her, gently stroking her hair. "Sleep," Robert whispered, kissing Alicia.

"Yes, sleep," said Melep, slipping an arm around Alicia. "Sleep if you can. Either way, we are here. And *we* are real."

"Yes," Alicia whispered, enfolded in warmth and comfort. "Yes, you are."

12. Support

The next day, Alicia suspended her catch-up work with the SSI to join Sharon and the others for a meeting of the support group. The need to be among others sharing her predicament, to some degree at least, was too great to resist. The group gathered twice a week, in the morning, in one of the numerous outdoor cafes to be found in a Commonwealth-style habitat. There were eleven participants, counting Sharon and Alicia, eight Human and three Leyra'an; the Human participants had all met Alicia in Simone's clinic when they'd been set up for monitoring. The matter was discussed freely, all of those suffering the odd memory hoard malfunction more than willing to haul their strange dreams out into the light of the real world.

"It makes them somehow a little less real,"

said a man named Jason.

"That takes some doing," Alicia replied. "I remember mine like they were part of yesterday's events."

"Same here," said the woman directly across the table from Alicia. She had visible Asian ancestry and a name – Chyou – to match. "It's actually gotten confusing from time to time."

"Well, yes, to be honest, that's happened to me as well," Jason said.

"But it helps a great deal to know we aren't alone with this problem," said Alejandro. "Although I fear it might subvert the purpose of the group."

"Don't worry about that," Sharon said. "We all have different versions of problems stemming from the war, and the losses we endured. Talk about what needs to be talked about." Everyone voiced agreement with that idea.

For the most part they sat quietly drinking coffee, tea, or Leyra'an *mi'pat*, talking about those they'd lost and their own experiences during the brief time the Faceless War had come to Pr'pri System. Listening to their accounts, and sharing their tears, Alicia began to see something else she had in common with the other monitor participants. She brought that up after a lull in the conversation, as people sat sipping their prefered beverages and eating the pastries the group had earlier agreed would be a fine idea.

"So, you two were in combat armor, same

as me, when the device was fired?" Alicia asked.

Alejandro nodded, and a woman named Abebe said, "I was."

"The two of us were working as medics," said Chyou, with a gesture toward Jason. "Same suit systems, minus heavy weapons."

"I was suited for emergency tech response," Burt added. "The mechanic's edition of powered armor. Not unarmed."

"Me too," said Hakim. "And yes, same suit tech, but with minimal weaponry, kitted out for rapid response to life support system damage."

"Well, that is the explanation for why you survived at all, so close to the device," said a Leyra'an named Tyk'ital Rewn. "Or so I've heard."

"It is," Alicia said. "And for that reason, I find it difficult to believe that it's merely a coincidence that those of us experiencing this memory hoard malfunction all just happen to have been in some form of powered EVA or combat gear."

"Some sort of accidental interface with the suit's systems and the hoard?" Burt asked.

"Driven by the immense EM pulse that went along with the detonation," Alicia replied with a nod. "I'll suggest that to Simone today."

"We surely weren't the only people suited up at the time," Abebe said.

"Simone should investigate that," Hakim agreed with a nod. "It would be good to be ready for them when they are awakened."

The conversation drifted away from their

specific experiences, and back once again to the reason for which the group had gathered. It was a morning well spent from Alicia's point of view. When Sharon said the time had come to go their separate ways, Alicia gathered the other six monitor participants and told them of the celebration taking place at the Willow Lake Inn that very evening. "My family is hosting this, to celebrate my survival and restoration," she explained. "We've all come back from the same injury. Join us, and bring whoever you like." To the three Leyra'an she said, "And you too. Why not? The more, the merrier."

"I believe I will," Chyou replied, and the others nodded and smiled in response to the idea.

"That goes for you, too," Alicia said, as she and Sharon made their way to the nearest tram stop.

"Thanks," Sharon replied. "I'll be there."

On their way to the SSI, Alicia contacted Ira Ashe, proprietor of the Willow Lake Inn, to warn him of the increased guest list. He thanked her for the update, and assured her it presented no problems.

At the Institute, she accompanied Sharon to Simone's clinic, having decided the sooner they talked about the ideas that had been shared by her fellow survivors, the better. Simone listened and, when Alicia was done, raised an eyebrow. "An accidental interface between the suit and the hoard – yes, that's definitely worth investigating. Especially now that we've got another ten survivors healed well enough to awaken. I've got them in a stable condition, holding steady until we know what's going on with the seven of you. If there's a connection between suit tech and the hoard malfunction, we want that nailed down before we revive anyone else who fits your parameters."

"These were suit wearers, then?" Alicia asked.

Simone nodded and said, "And all ten of them have blocked memory hoards, same as the seven of you wearing the monitors right now."

Sharon was studying a pale green dataframe. "I've got a data catcher searching everything in the records connected to the neural links and what they registered while the seven of you were in the suits. And..." She flicked her fingers back and forth within the frame, "I'm setting up a filter to find out who else was wearing a suit at the time of the Pulsar detonation. Let's see how strongly that correlates to memory hoard lock-up."

"Good idea," said Simone. "If the correlation proves strong enough, it would certainly support our current line of inquiry."

"I hope something turns up," said Alicia. "It certainly would make what I'm experiencing worth the stress, if it means no one else needs to endure it."

"Pretty sure the others would agree with you," said Sharon.

"We need to look at records of the dataflow between the habitat systems and the suits,"

Simone mused. "That's a lot of data. Possibly enough, if it were misdirected, to overload a hoard."

"In the short time the Pulsar had to mess things up?" Sharon wondered.

Simone opened a new dataframe, flicked her fingers through the glowing text within, and then enlarged a number in exponential notation. "That's the average data flow in petabytes under normal circumstances."

Sharon cleared her throat and said, "Yes, well, that certainly makes this seem a promising line of investigation."

"That's for damned sure," Alicia said as she rose. Having accomplished her purpose in this visit, she wanted to get some work done. "Let me know if I can be of any further help."

"You're wearing monitors," Sharon said. "Right now, it's data we need, so that's help."

With a grimace, Alicia said, "I'm hoping I won't be able to provide any tonight. I need a good night's sleep."

"Well, the party tonight should put you in the right frame of mind," Simone said. "Tonight's the night, right?"

"It is," Alicia replied. "So, I'll see you both later."

Alicia went to her office, but instead of her planned work, she called up tech manuals for the combat armor she'd worn the day the war ended. The irony of their current thinking was inescapable. The suits had saved their lives when the Pulsar went off and disabled the Faceless. But the suits may also have caused the damage that so bedeviled them in the present time. With the specs up in a dataframe, she summoned comparable manuals for the sorts of reinforced suits worn by med techs and by those assigned to emergency repairs in hazardous situations. They were, indeed, remarkable in their similarity. All were constructed from near impervious articulated armor, with an interior that molded itself to the user. All designs were self-contained, with environmental and recycling systems, sanitary maintenance, and consumables capable of sustaining the wearer for three days. Onboard computers were linked through a multiply redundant comm system to maintain contact with a base of operations. All the designs also included, in the comm package, a permanently open link that provided base or squadron commanders with telemetry on the condition of a given suit's occupant.

The medical data in the data stream came from the nanomed interface included in all memory hoards. The system could send and receive, through that open link, a capacity that only increased her suspicion that this component of the system might be the conduit.

A permanently open link. That almost certainly played a roll. She added that thought to the brief review she was putting together for Simone's use.

Among the layers of protection offered by such suits was a powerful electromagnetic field, modulated in a way to avoid interference with communications, and yet strong enough to neutralize the EM pulse emitted by a powerful stellar flare, or a nearby nuclear detonation. Simone and Tuleselan were both convinced that the combination of this field with the nonconductive armor was the reason suit wearers near the SSI were injured – some badly – but not killed outright by the detonation of the Pulsar weapon.

Alicia's suit was one of two that had been heavily armed; she had carried the full tactical kit into the fight – for all the good it had done. She checked that derisive thought, realizing as she did that the fire she had unleashed on the enemy had held them off just long enough. Without it, she would have been taken. Instead, she had lived long enough to endure the Pulsar, as it disrupted the offensive capability of the Faceless. It was an amazing thing to contemplate, that anyone at all had survived a twisting of local space-time so severe that the nearby trans-spacial node had collapsed. For a moment, she wished she could still see that battle in her memory, but the moment quickly passed. Whether Jeanine thought it was a good idea or not, Alicia was in no hurry to have the memory of witnessing Holm's death brought out of sequestration.

She made a few more notes, bundled them with the technical specifications she had harvested, and sent the data packet off to Simone. Alicia was cautiously optimistic that somewhere in all of this, they would find at least part of their answer.

The door to her office chimed softly and

she opened it with a word. Two slim, ebony Nesvama, in shimmery green and rose pastel robes respectively, entered. Their hair crests matched their garments in color. "Tuleselan," Alicia said in greeting to her colleague. And then to his green-clad wife, "Peralasen. It's so good to see you. I'd heard you arrived yesterday."

"It is good to be back," Peralasen replied with the chest-high hand-clasp gesture used by members of the old Concordance as a sign of greeting. "And very good to see you awake at last. You are well, I am to understand?"

"Physically healthy," Alicia said. She tapped the side of her head and added, "Have some things to work out up here, but..."

"Indeed," Peralasen said. "Two years is a considerable gap to bridge."

"Well, yes, that too."

"We are on our way to your gathering at the Willow Lake Inn," said Tuleselan. "Could we convince you to travel there with us?"

"That sounds good to me," Alicia replied, waving away the remaining dataframes and getting up from behind her desk. "Give me a couple of minutes. I want to change into something more casual."

"We will wait right here," Peralasen assured her.

Alicia went into the private quarters connected with her office and dressed Leyra'an style, with a snug blouse of deep rust red, a short green jacket, and a long loose green skirt. Across her chest, at a diagonal, was the braided *es'ava* that twined together the colors – gold, green, and bright blue – of house Rost'aht.

"You wear the styles of your adoptive people very well," said Peralasen when Alicia rejoined them.

"Thanks."

Alicia led them to the nearest lift terminus and set the Willow Lake Inn as their destination. The time for the gathering was at hand, and didn't leave time enough to use her preferred way to travel. The network of lift tubes that laced the inner hull of the habitat, extending into larger building complexes such as the SSI, would make the trip in a fraction of the time a tram took. She'd intended to leave earlier, but had become preoccupied with her investigation of powered armor suits. It would not be the first time Alicia had been a late arrival because work had so absorbed her mind. In this case, the lapse would do no harm, and had provided the benefit of good traveling companions. Alicia let the translation system render Nesvama speech understandable, but listened with pleasure to the musical sounds of their voices. She understood some of the language, and had every intention of one day being able to understand Nesvama as easily as she did Leyra'an.

She would never speak it, though. The Human mouth and vocal cords lacked the range and flexibility of the Nesvama counterparts.

They discussed her current situation and Peralasen, herself a member of the SSI research staff, wondered aloud if a clue might be found studying possible feedback signals generated when the weapon had rippled space-time. "It may be more complicated than mere data overload," she pointed out. "The Pulsar would have warped the signals being sent and received."

"It would seem a factor worthy of investigation," said Tuleselan.

"I agree," Alicia said.

"I could set up a search for records of spurious signals in the comm system, at the moment the detonation took place," Peralasen said.

"Surely those records were scrambled when the field was released," said Alicia.

"No doubt," Tuleselan replied. "But a remarkable amount of data stored by habitat onboard systems survived in backup format."

"Can't hurt to look," Alicia admitted.

"No," said Peralasen. "It surely cannot. With your permission, I will examine the matter."

"Please, feel free," Alicia said, smiling a Leyra'an smile. "We need all the help we can get."

They moved on to less serious matters, family news and stories of offspring misbehavior, something the Sibling Species all had in common – except for the Grahlin, who as clones had no offspring, and were decanted near adulthood in any case. The Nesvama family had increased by one, while Alicia was unconscious, and in part because Nesvama children grew and matured more rapidly than Human children, they had plenty of tales to tell of their child's first two years.

"Sounds like Ritafanin is quite the handful, all by itself," Alicia said. She could not specify gender in her comments, since Nesvama were genderless until their late teens, at which time they decided between male and female, developing accordingly afterward. She hated saying "it" with regards to their child, but knew the translator would render "it" as the correct gender-neutral Nesvama word.

"Oh, indeed," said Tuleselan.

"We would have it no other way," Peralasen assured her.

"I can certainly relate to that." And so, Alicia in turn gave them a quick account of her quiet adventure winning over the daughter of Holm and Melep. Sadness was expressed by her companions that the little girl would know her father only as images and a story based on the memories of others. Alicia quietly agreed with the sentiment, and let it go at that.

"The children, and this includes Nol'ez Jaxi, are looking forward to seeing Ritafanin tonight," she said, moving on to a happier subject. "They expect it to be brimming with stories about the trip the two of you took," meaning Ritafanin and its mother.

"Oh, they will not be disappointed," Peralasen replied.

This Alicia did not doubt. The Nesvama had a natural talent for telling stories.

The lift capsule slowed and stopped,

opening to release them into a part of the habitat very familiar to Alicia's eyes.

13. Willow Lake Inn

The lift station was perched on a grassy hilltop, with the station proper surrounded by a pavement of dark, fitted stone. The gentle, grass-covered slope before them was liberally sprinkled with the blossoms of pink clover, and stingless bumblebees went about their business from blossom to blossom. The flagstone pavement at the foot of the station joined a pair of pathways, also paved with fitted stones. One path headed around to the other side of the hill; the second path was the one that would lead them the rest of the way to their destination. Alicia walked the path flanked by her Nesvama friends, feeling a touch melancholy thinking of the path in a probeship these stones once paved, and those now lost who once had walked along it.

Not the mood you need right now. She

drew a deep breath, relishing the scent of grass and the blooming lilacs that dotted the slope. The great axial lamp still shed the full light of a summer afternoon. Not that it was ever not summer here. The melancholy feelings faded away.

And so she was smiling when she walked with her friends over the wide stone bridge that crossed the inflow stream for mirror-smooth Willow Lake. It was well named for the stately weeping willows growing around it, their long branches just touching the water. A scattering of waterfowl, including a pair of swans, swam calmly across the lake. Over the bridge, and there was the eponymous inn, built of stone and with wooden shingles, a faithful replica of an establishment of the sort that would have served travelers in a long-ago time, on a world called Earth. A world Alicia had never seen, something that was not at all unusual for the majority of the Human population. The inn was identical to the one in which Robert had courted her aboard the probeship *William Bartram*, back when they both served the Commonwealth Survey.

No, not just identical. It's the same structure. We brought every bit of it over here, and then reassembled it.

It had been removed from the wrecked probeship when the material of the *William Bartram* was salvaged and recycled into the construction of this habitat that would share its name, a living memorial to a great ship and its tragic fate. Many aspects of the probeship had been recovered in that way, and it was here within the Bartram habitat that most of the survivors yet lived.

Alicia led them down to where the stone path met the patio that stretched from the front of the building to the lake shore. The patio was paved with the same sort of dark asteroidal stone as the path. Tables and chairs were set around the edge of the patio, leaving the middle portion open for the inevitable dancing. There was a stage near the front of the inn. Her family and a number of friends were there already, including several Nesvama who had Ritafanin in their care. The youngling darted toward its parents, leaving behind the four other children in attendance – the Rost'aht boys, Sylvia, and Nol'ez Jaxi – and making chirping sounds that Alicia assumed were indicative of happiness. Certainly her friends appeared pleased, with Tuleselan sweeping his child up and resting it in the crook of one long, black arm.

"You are Alicia Rost'aht-MacGregor," said Ritafanin.

"That's me," she replied with a smile. "You may call me Alicia."

"I am most honored to meet you." The Nesvama child made the handclasp gesture of a Member of the Grand Concordance.

Alicia responded in kind, then bowed in the stiff-backed Leyra'an fashion. "The honor is mutual," she said. "Very pleased to meet you."

"I am a friend of your sons and your daughter," Ritafanin informed her as they made their way onto the patio. "Also of the one named Jaxi. I missed them greatly when I traveled."

"The feeling was mutual," Alicia said. "They were glad to know you had returned home safely." She worked not to show amusement at the child's serious demeanor.

It quickly became clear that Ritafanin was becoming restless at being held. "I should return to my companions."

"I believe that would be the proper thing to do," said Tuleselan, who stooped and set his child down. "Rejoin us for the meal."

"I shall." And the youngling Nesvama darted away in a swirl of child-sized pastel orange Nesvama robes.

"Ritafanin is adorable," Alicia told her friends.

"We are in agreement," said Peralasen.

They followed the child to a pair of long tables at the edge of the patio, looking out over the lake. There the trio halted and watched as Ritafanin sprinted to the lake shore, eager to catch up with the other children who were now at the water's edge. Highlights from the axial lamp's illumination glinted in the wake of paddling ducks and geese. The Nesvama couple and Alicia were greeted by a chorus of voices. Although most of the guests were Human, the full range of Sibling Species was indeed represented. Around the tables, in chairs appropriate for sizes and shapes, were diminutive gray-clad Grahlin, Leyra'an with colorful *es'avas*, Hroom of fur either dark or light, and Nesvama who, taken together, resembled a soft rainbow. Also among the invitees were a yellow-skinned Rusalas couple in their form-fitting garments of many swirling colors, and a quartet of insectoid T'lack researchers who Alicia knew from the Institute.

Seeing such an assemblage once again brought to mind the image of her weary doppelgänger. The Alicia of the First Iteration could not know that her work had not only saved Humanity, but had created something of surpassing beauty in this corner of the galaxy. And that creation had made it possible for the T'lack, who were anything *but* a direct result of that creation, to become one of Humanity's best friends and allies. She knew, as did they all, that the Faceless War would have come to a very different end, had the T'lack not first encountered the Sibling Species known as the Rusalas.

Once again, she directed a wish to that exhausted, frightened, despairing version of herself, and then wished there were some way the woman could know how successful she had been. *I will always remember you,* she said to that other version of herself. *I owe you and yours so much. I owe you everything!*

"Welcome back, Alicia," someone shouted. A tall man with thick, black hair, wearing a white apron over brown coveralls, approached her with a large mug that she knew would be filled with the best beer in the galaxy.

"Hello, Ira," she said to the proprietor of the Willow Lake Inn. She took the mug and planted a kiss on his cheek. “And hello to all of you,” she added, saluting them with the mug before taking a long drink. And it certainly was the best brew of them all. Alicia was glad she’d thought to dial back her nanomed response to alcohol.

Looking around, she saw that Simone and Sharon were just then walking onto the patio, with the other six patients trailing along behind; the Leyra’an members of the support group had arrived ahead of Alicia. “Over here!” she called to them, as if they wouldn’t have navigated into the correct orbit on their own. And navigate they did, joining the crowd and soon adding to the noise level. The party proper was at the pair of lakeside tables, but anyone who showed up for an evening at the inn was soon drawn in to some degree. The habitat’s ceilidh band – an eclectic group of Leyra’an and Human musicians with fiddles, an accordion, guitars, a bodhran, and flutes – set up on one side of the patio and added Celtic tunes both ancient and recently composed in the same style. Two of the songs were by Robert, as it happened. People were soon dancing as well as eating and drinking. When the words to a tune were known, one or more in attendance sang, or sang along with the band, with varying degrees of quality.

A gaggle of children raced around the shores of the lake, or improvised dances of their own. Their number had been increased to nearly a dozen by the offspring of other guests; led by Nol’ez Jaxi, they were accompanied by an assortment of canines and han'angas. Shrill voices frequently rose above the music and conversation, rising suddenly to higher notes when someone fell into the lake. It was a frequent occurrence, and Alicia doubted it was ever entirely accidental – or malicious. Parents looked out to where the hijinks took place, but there was no sign of worry. The lake was actually very shallow, children of Bartram were routinely taught how to swim, and both dogs and han'angas were well trained in the rescue of floundering children.

Alicia danced with her husband, with Ira, with Simone, and with other men and women, some of whom she knew and others she met that night for the first time. She ate well, imbibed to just beyond the detox level set for her nanomed, sang with the band once, and nearly fell into the lake herself when Vurn and Paul drew her into a game of tag. She was the only adult to be tempted into the game. The only adult Human, that is. The Grahlin in attendance, being of a stature similar to the older children, proved to be adept at games that involved sprinting around. At least two of them ended up in the water. They emerged sodden, but laughing.

Much of the shadow of grief and loss that had clung to her since awakening was banished that night. It was as if the party drew a line between those things and the here-and-now.

The evening was well along before she realized no one from the Milhouse family had turned up. Alicia was quietly mortified that it had taken her so long to realize this, and in fact it was Simone who brought the matter to her attention.

"I was under the impression your friend would join us," she said, at a moment when the band was taking a break and the noise level permitted easy conversation.

"I did expect Jeanine to be here," Alicia replied. "I have no idea what changed her plan. I hope it wasn't the family crisis."

"Well, this party isn't exactly over," Simone pointed out. "She may yet make it. I'm looking forward to meeting her."

And so Alicia kept an eye open for the next hour, and when Jeanine failed to arrive, went into the inn proper for the quiet and privacy she needed to make a call. The comm system responded with a Do Not Disturb icon in a pale blue dataframe. That it was in blue prevented her from feeling any worry; orange or red would have meant the family was in the midst of a crisis or emergency. Alicia still went back out into the party feeling concerned about her friend. It wasn't like Jeanine, or her family for that matter, to miss a party of this sort. But as soon as she returned she found herself swept into another dance by her husband, and the matter, while not quite forgotten, became a less immediate concern.

The light from the axial lamp slowly dimmed and twilight came to the Bartram habitat, the long, slow fade from day into night as it would happen in midsummer on distant Earth. The resident population of fireflies began to wink on and off, not quite muted by the crystalline lights of many colors strung around and over the patio. Light from the windows of the inn spilled out, soft and golden.

Energy levels in the partiers began to fade; fewer danced and, perhaps mercifully, fewer sang. Children were chasing fireflies, or sleeping off large meals in the soft grass of the low hills around the lake. Alicia was sipping wine, sitting back and taking it all in, enjoying the flow of conversation going on around her. The mood was relaxed and comfortable.

She went off to the darkness under the nearest willow, activated the comm system, and requested a line open to the Milhouse residence. The same icon, surrounded by a shimmering blue aura, was all she received.

Simone looked up at her as she returned. "Any word from your friend?" she asked.

Alicia shook her head. "Comm still gives me a Do Not Disturb icon."

"That doesn't sound like the Milhouses," Robert observed.

"It's unusual," Alicia admitted. "But they're having an unpleasant visit from Greg's parents. No way those two would come here and join *this* party. And I doubt the Milhouses would be so rude as to just abandon his parents for the evening." But even as she spoke, Alicia wondered why Jeanine would not have sent a message that they would be absent.

"Still trying to save their souls?" Robert asked.

"So she says," Alicia replied. "Greg's

brother and sister-in-law are already on their way home, angry and defiant, according to Jeanine. But Greg's parents are still here, apparently being a problem."

"I wonder if Greg had a relapse?" Robert said.

"Relapse?" Sharon asked.

"After Sylvia's death, he had trouble coping," Robert explained. "We were all worried sick, to be honest. Jeanine was afraid he would do something rash."

"Suicide?" Simone guessed.

Beside her, Sharon grimaced. "It's rare for that to happen among Commonwealth Humans," she said. "But not unheard of."

"Greg Milhouse isn't Commonwealth," Alicia said. "He grew up in the Republic."

"Oh."

"Well, the system isn't registering anything like an emergency," Alicia said. "But if he's having that kind of trouble, I can see where Jeanine and Becca might have their hands full. Though it's odd that she didn't mention anything of the sort to me when we talked the other day."

"That is odd," said Robert. "You two talk about everything, it seems."

"We usually do," Alicia agreed. "But she made it sound like Greg was holding his own. If this visit caused a setback, it may not be something she wants others to know about."

"Can't blame her for that," said Sharon.

The party eventually settled down to a quiet gathering of a few close friends, until late that night it was down to her family and that of Nol'ez. The Nol'ez family joined them for the return home by tram, since their residence was only a short walk from that of Rost'aht. Jaxi walked along between John and Wirolen, the lack of skip in her step revealing her weariness. Vurn and Paul appeared to be sleepwalking, kept on the path by Melep and the ever-attentive Gava'mi. Robert carried Sylvia, who was dead to the world. They said good night to the Nol'ez family and prepared for a good night's sleep.

Alicia snuggled with her partners, and quiet things were said of their delight in how the evening had gone, and of the love they shared. That they were three instead of four was always there, but in that moment they all knew it was a thought best left unspoken. She felt more relaxed than she had since she'd left the habitat's infirmary. There seemed no reason to doubt that she would, this night at least, have a good night's sleep.

14. Unreality

Growing daylight woke her, and Alicia stretched, reveling in the feeling of being well rested. Robert and Melep were up already, but this happened as often as not, Alicia being anything but an early riser. It was a quiet morning, with only the song of a distant mockingbird drifting through the window. The endlessly inventive song of the bird made her smile. Alicia rose and headed for the bathroom. After her morning ablutions, she made her way downstairs to the main family room on the ground floor.

All was quiet, but it was soon apparent that this was not simply a peaceful morning. It was abnormally quiet for a household containing a trio of rambunctious siblings and an energetic han'anga. A growing uneasiness moved her through the house with ever greater haste. Alicia went into the kitchen, and found it unoccupied. With bewilderment quickly rising to anxiety, and then alarm, she went back upstairs and checked the rooms of their children, and then up to the open-air third floor. Everywhere she looked she saw the signs of ordinary daily activity: scattered clothing and toys left by careless children, with half-empty mugs of *mi'pat* – stone cold – on the upstairs table, and Gava'mi's half-eaten morning meal in the kitchen. To all appearances, her family had simply, suddenly, vanished in the midst of the normal morning routine.

"Robert?" she called out. "Melep!" In a louder voice.

No one answered.

Alicia hurried downstairs and out the front door, looking around for any sign of her family. The mockingbird sang on and the ducks swam peacefully in the pond near their home, but there wasn't a sign of her Human or Leyra'an neighbors. This, at a time when people would surely be up and about. Her fear gathering strength, Alicia began to run toward the Nol'ez residence – and stopped herself.

"Oh, *hell* no," she groaned. "Not again."

Realizing this was yet another lucid dream, she once again called up the mental exercises Jeanine had taught her, hoping that this time they would have the desired effect. As she controlled her breathing and heart rate – hoping all the while this would be reflected in her unconscious physical body – she felt the desired calm settle into place. She closed her eyes and let that sense of calm and control fill her. Opening them, she saw with a twinge of annoyance that nothing had changed.

An idea occurred. She made her way back to the house and stretched out on one of the lounge chairs within sight of their kitchen garden and small vineyard. They grew only table grapes, and as she looked at the vines, Alicia saw that they were nearly ripe. With a sigh, she closed her eyes and relaxed, imagining the taste of fresh grapes.

"What are you doing out here?" Robert asked.

Alicia sat up, yawning, then fought back the sudden impulse to throw off the bed clothes and clutch him to her. She wanted to maintain that feeling of being calm and in control. But they weren't in bed. Instead, she sat up and set her bare feet in the grass. "Oh, no," she whispered. "Now I'm sleepwalking." She leaned forward, her face in her hands, anything but calm.

From behind, she heard children talking and laughing and the shrill warble of an excited han'anga; they were giving Gava'mi his breakfast. She heard Melep's usual admonition to stay down; Gava'mi was generally well behaved, but breakfast always brought the pup out in him.

"Sleepwalking?" Robert asked, sitting beside her.

"I woke up, or thought I did," she explained, sitting up to look at him. "There was no one here. I mean no one, anywhere. I came outside, trying to find out what was going on, and I started to panic. That's when I realized it had to be one of those damned dreams. So I used one of Jeanine's biofeedback tricks, and stretched out to relax where I found myself. Fell asleep, but – I didn't wake back up in bed."

"This is not a step in the right direction," Robert said, one eyebrow raised.

"That's for damned sure." She took his hand and he returned the grip firmly. "Comm, Dr. Simone Newcomb. Accept visual."

To all appearances, Simone's office opened up on the grass between them and the garden. "Good morning," Simone said, saluting them with her coffee mug. The image was so realistic they could see steam rising from the coffee. "What's up?"

Suddenly, Alicia wanted coffee in the worst way. "I am, and not in a way that makes me happy. I had another lucid dream." She described the experience to Simone. "When Robert woke me, I was still out here, on a lounger, right where I went back to sleep in the dream."

"Somnambulism?" Simone's voice and expression were equally eloquent in displaying her surprise. A flock of dataframes unfolded around her, and each was given a quick appraisal. "That hasn't happened to the others, at least, not yet."

"I half expected your alarm to go off again," Alicia said.

Simone diminished all but one of the dataframes. "There's a blip, but it's only a tick or two above the level of a normal dream, and it didn't sustain... Ah, of course. The biofeedback."

"It must have settled me down before I went off the chart," Alicia concluded. "That's not a complaint."

"I think you're right," Simone said with a nod. "I need to examine the data on a finer scale. Maybe this change will give us a clue. You said it wasn't as chaotic as the others?"

"Not at all," Alicia replied. "Everything otherwise seemed perfectly normal. What frightened me was finding my family had apparently vanished in an instant, while doing their normal morning routine."

"That you could recognize your situation and take constructive action is encouraging," Simone said. "But it also deepens the mystery of what exactly is happening to you."

"You said no one else has had a similar experience?" Robert asked.

"Not yet." Simone scrolled quickly through a data stream, then shook her head and frowned. "Looks like everyone had their sleep disturbed, some deeply, but nothing like the one that woke all of us up the other night. So far, no one has checked in, except you, so I don't have any dream descriptions."

"Is this sleepwalking anything dangerous, in and of itself?" Robert asked.

"Under some circumstances, it could be risky," Simone replied. "People sometimes injure themselves while sleepwalking, and I'm not at all sure what the effect would have been had one of you interacted with her in that state." She peered closely at her dataframe, then nodded. "Okay, I think I have a way to manage this safely, if it happens again. The data flow clearly shows motor control centers in your brain engaging at the same time this dream came on. I'll program the system to alert Robert and Melep if this combination of patterns repeats. They can stay nearby and watch over you, to keep you safe until you wake up."

"Thanks," said Alicia. "That makes me feel better."

"Anything I can do to help, my friend," said Simone. "I will do it. And – ah, one of your fellow dreamers is calling in."

"Go ahead and take that call," Alicia said. "I think we're okay here."

The projected office vanished, restoring the view of the garden and the vines beyond. "Those grapes are pretty close to ready, aren't they?" Alicia asked.

"As a matter of fact, they are," he replied.

"Good. I'd like to make some grape jam with part of this harvest." She kissed him and rose to her feet. "Right now, I need breakfast. And coffee. Oh, do I ever need..."

Alicia woke up, with the first light of day streaming through the bedroom window. A mockingbird sang lustily outside, and her husband was beside her on the bed, propped on one elbow, smiling gently.

"Melep just called up from the kitchen," he said. "Breakfast is about ready."

"Oh." Alicia groaned and rolled onto her back, eyes locked on the ceiling. "Oh, *shit!*"

15. Perchance To Dream

Later that morning, sitting across the desk from Simone in the doctor's office, Alicia said again, "Shit."

"No kidding."

"How can that *possibly* be right?"

Simone shook her head, obviously as baffled and unhappy as Alicia felt. "There's got to be a glitch in the monitor program. Somewhere. But the normal diagnostic programs aren't finding it." Letting go an exasperated sigh, she said, "I need an Artificial to look into this. The Library Annex might be able to help. But this is beyond my understanding. I don't even know how to start."

It was in the nature of this dataframe that they could both read it, from either side. And so both of them were peering up at the gently glowing graphic display as they spoke. Simone's field of medicine was not one in which Alicia had much experience, but she had expanded her knowledge enough over the decades – the celebration of her first century was only a couple of years ahead – that she could draw understanding from what she saw.

"So, while I was dreaming within a dream, my motor function fired off. That's not unusual for a dream, but this..." and with the tip of her finger she highlighted one line of data. "This metabolic function data clearly reads that my leg muscles were supporting my full weight. That can only mean I was up and walking around at *some* point, even if I did finally wake up in bed."

If I really woke up then. Gaia, am I awake now? She did not say it aloud.

The thought frankly horrified her, and with a shudder Alicia quickly turned away from it. It lingered in the back of her mind, a tiny whisper of anxiety, even though she worked to convince herself that it was too absurd to contemplate. Simone was saying something about a link between the metabolic data and a neurological data point, but her voice faded away, overridden by – something else.

"To die, to sleep
To sleep perchance to dream:
Ay, there's the rub.
For in that sleep of death what dreams

may come...”

It was a voice, out loud, right beside her. One she knew and loved, and for which she yet grieved.

No! For a moment she couldn’t breathe. *No!* Denial was a monstrous thing, stuffed into that tiny word.

“Alicia? *Hey!*”

Simone was suddenly there beside the chair, grabbing her shoulders to keep her from toppling over. Alicia could sense her presence and feel a firm grip holding her upright, but she couldn’t see Simone. Her vision had tunneled, locked on the dataframe over Simone’s desk; it pulsed with light and the outer frame seemed to stretch and shrink. In the background could be heard the shrill tone of a nanomed alarm, signaling a crisis-level intervention in progress. And something was pulling on her, inside her head. The feeling was as uncanny as it was uncomfortable.

She covered her face with her hands, hunched over, and wept. Grief she’d thought under control surged through her and, much as it hurt, there was no diverting it. No denying it. She had heard him, as if he’d been in the room beside her. Through it all, Simone held on to her, saying nothing. The alarm ceased its shrilling call, and Alicia felt her heartbeat slow to normal as the nanomed pushed her various hormone levels and blood pressure back to her normal baseline. A few moments later, she took a deep breath and sat up straight. Simone gave her shoulder a squeeze, and looked up at the dataframe, which pulsed with data – and warnings.

"Gaia," Simone whispered. "It shows you slipping into REM sleep and back out, all in a moment."

"That's not possible," Alicia whispered, shaking her head and sniffing. Her body felt chilled, and she was trembling. "I'm right here with you. Awake. Or am I? Oh, Gaia, Mother of All Life..."

"You're awake," Simone asserted. "Because otherwise I'm a dream element, a hallucination, and frankly, I feel *way* too self-conscious at the moment for that to be the case." She was still studying the display, scrolling and flicking data points into and out of view with quick, practiced touches of one slender finger. "What the hell is *this?* Activity in your auditory cortex spiked for a moment. As if someone spoke sharply into one ear."

"Someone did," said Alicia.

"Someone – who? Damn it, there's just the two of us here."

"Holm," Alicia muttered.

"Alicia..."

"I know. *I know!*" She clutched at the armrests of her chair as a wave of vertigo swept through her, threatening to tumble her to the floor. "Holm is dead. But it was – *him*. It was Holm. *I heard him!*" Alicia held her breath and clenched her teeth, struggling not to step over the edge into hysteria. The alarms were beeping again; she was presenting the nanomed with a challenge.

Simone gave her a moment, then asked, "What did he say?"

"Shakespeare," Alicia replied. "He quoted Shakespeare. Hamlet. To die, to sleep. To sleep perchance to dream, aye, there's the rub.'" She paused and drew a shaky breath and went on in a whisper, looking up at Simone. "For in that sleep of death what dreams may come..."

"Alicia, listen to me." Simone knelt in front of Alicia's chair and pried her hands loose, clasping them between hers. "And look at me. That was a hallucination. An auditory hallucination. Something your unconscious mind dragged up."

"Simone, I'm scared."

"I don't blame you."

"What the hell is happening to me?"

"I wish I could be sure," Simone replied. She sighed and shook her head. "This is beyond anything I've treated or studied. Dreams within dreams, there's precedent for that. Hallucinations, those too. But you seem to be slipping in and out of dream states without any warning." She stood up, looking frustrated and shaking her head again. "That much is right there in the data, and can't be denied. The triggering mechanism – is the mystery."

"We can't stop any of this until that mystery is resolved."

"No," Simone replied. "We can't."

"Jeanine is adamant that the block on my memory hoard, the one still functional, needs to be removed," Alicia said. "She's concerned that the conflict between my simply knowing

Holm is dead, and not being able to deal with the experience, could have serious consequences."

"You're thinking these disturbances might be such a consequence?"

"A wild guess," Alicia admitted. "But right now I'm trying to snatch pebbles out of a decaying orbit. We've got to try something!"

"We should check it out, definitely," Simone said. "If it isn't the direct cause, it may be complicating matters. But I want this friend of yours with us before we do anything."

"Let's see what she's up to," Alicia suggested. "She may have gotten things settled at home by now. Comm, connect to Jeanine Milhouse." An instant later a dataframe appeared beside the one being used by Simone, a blue Do Not Disturb icon at its heart. Seeing that icon yet again brought a sudden sense of uneasiness. "Comm, override DND. This is an emergency." The icon flashed, then was replaced by a message that the override had received no response. "Locate Jeanine Milhouse."

Unable to comply.

"Locate Gregory Milhouse and Rebecca Milhouse."

Unable to comply.

"That's bizarre," said Simone. "If any of them are anywhere in the habitat, their nanomed signal would locate them."

"His parents were trying to force them to leave." Something cold seemed to close in around Alicia's heart. "System welfare check,

Milhouse residence."

Even as she spoke, the blue data frame flipped and turned red. *Medical emergency,* was the new message. *Emergency medical assistance sent.*

"No," Alicia whispered. "No, please tell me I'm dreaming again."

"Come on," said Simone, as she pulled Alicia up from the chair and rushed out of her office.

They hurried to a nearby lift station, where Simone used her medical credentials to summon an emergency reroute of an express capsule, citing a response to the situation discovered at the Milhouse residence. It was necessary to strap in, and Alicia felt herself pressed back into the couch by the sudden acceleration used by a lift capsule in emergency mode. Ahead, she knew, other travelers were being shunted into holding locations to permit the rapid passage.

It still seemed to take a horribly long time to reach the portion of the habitat in which the Milhouses lived.

They arrived all too soon, considering what awaited them. A dozen men and women, a mixture of Humans and Leyra'an, were already on the scene. The front door of the modest structure — a single-story adobe-style building surrounded by well tended gardens — stood open. The Humans were all pale and shaken; the Leyra'an had the dark shading around their eyes that indicated grief or fear.

"You don't want to go in there," said a

Human woman clad in the dark blue uniform of habitat Security.

"Why?" Simone demanded.

Alicia found it impossible to speak. Dread filled her, requiring no knowledge to feed its existence.

"They're dead," was the reply. The woman shuddered. She spoke barely above a whisper. "Gaia. All of them. Killed..." She turned away and left them at a quick walk. A moment later, they heard someone being violently ill.

Alicia walked through the door, compelled to do so, terrified as she was by what she had heard. She found herself in the living room, confronted by a sight she simply could not accept. For a heartbeat she felt the same flare of rage, such as she was sure she must have felt the moment she saw the Faceless overwhelm Holm. Then she was numb.

The Milhouses were slumped together on their sofa, each with an angry red hole burned through the forehead. Their eyes were open; they seemed startled. On the floor before them, almost at Alicia's feet as she stopped moving forward, was the body of a man dressed in conservative Republic style. The back of his head was gone. The muzzle of the gun he'd used to murder the Milhouses and then take his own life was still in his mouth.

16. Coping

"It was Greg's father," Robert said in a voice broken and hoarse. "His own father. They wouldn't return to the Republic, and so – he killed them. He even shot his own wife."

"How did he smuggle a gun into the habitat?" Melep demanded.

"He didn't," Robert replied. "It was Greg's. A wartime leftover." He was weeping again as he answered. The death of his friend was hitting him hard.

Alicia sat with her arm around her husband, going through the motions of offering comfort, but feeling numb. She found herself taking frequent, deep breaths, as if the oxygen content of the room was too low. "That weapon should have been locked out," she said between her teeth. "The system shouldn't have allowed it to go live. How? How the hell could this happen?"

"Old man Milhouse must have known a way around the safety protocol." Robert scrubbed a hand across his eyes. "Gaia! *I don't know*. But it hap – it happened."

Melep was looking at a system news dataframe, her eyes rimmed nearly black by her own tears. "The Bartram AI hasn't fully integrated with the habitat systems – it isn't completely awake and aware – but it detected the gun going active," she muttered half to herself. "According to the report, the Artificial was then locked out by the gun itself. Something that old man did, to be sure. The Artificial sounded an alarm, but..." She looked at Alicia and said, "Well, that's why emergency services already had the scene cordoned off when you got there."

"Why can't I wake up from this one?" Alicia whispered. "So many bad dreams, but *this* has to be real." She felt Robert slip his arms around her and draw her near; she leaned into the embrace, still numb and breathless with the emotional shock of what she had seen. Denial gripped her. It was impossible for such a thing to happen. People did not murder each other for any reason, let alone a refusal to give up their way of life. She knew history taught otherwise, but in modern times? In the Human Commonwealth? The Grand Concordance? Such things were unheard of.

Until now.

"I know the Republic is in turmoil," she muttered. "But enough to lead to such as this?"

"Apparently so," Robert replied, in a voice barely above a whisper.

Melep sat in the bowl-shaped Leyra'an chair called a *da'ouba* with her left arm around Robert's waist, still peering at the newsfeed, which slowly scrolled. "There's not much else here," she said softly. "Records of Greg's heroism in the war, grief expressed by the Bartram survivors that Jeanine – oh, gods of all clans..." Her voice choked off.

"What?" Alicia prompted when Melep did not continue.

"Rebecca. There was a boy. He – ah, the poor thing. He's under sedation. Not even the nanomed could control his reaction."

The numbness in her heart became a painful ache. Seeking something, anything, to break the spell, Alicia looked at the time stamp in the dataframe. "The children will be wanting dinner." It seemed an absurd non sequitur, but her heart was reaching for something, anything – else.

"I sent them over to the Nol'ez place," Melep replied. "John and Wirolen know what happened."

"Does Jaxi?" Alicia knew that Nol'ez Jaxi and Becca Milhouse had become more than close friends – Becca having taken on the role of older sister – over the two years Alicia had missed.

"I do not know," Melep said, her voice unsteady.

"We should join them," said Robert. "We should all be together to deal with this."

"Yes," said Melep. "In the Way of Leyra'an, that's as should be. Come." She assumed her role as matriarch of the household in a heartbeat, and gave them a center around which to regroup.

Robert and Alicia followed her without question. Such was the relationship between the two families that no one asked if the neighbors wanted their company. There was never any doubt in Alicia's mind as to the welcome they would receive. The three of them walked through the expanse of thick turf that spread between the two houses, their arms around each other. Wirolen appeared in the open doorway and held her arms out to them. Like Melep, the scales around her eyes had darkened from recent tears. Each was hugged tightly in turn, and then they were led into the family room with its cushioned Hroom-style central step pit. Four confused children and an anxious han'anga sat huddled together two steps down from the floor level, watching wide-eyed as the adults walked into the room. On the step above them sat John, watching over them. He rose and came forward to meet them, and more long embraces were exchanged.

"They know only that something bad has happened," said Wirolen. "We have not tried to explain it to them."

"Gaia," Alicia whispered. "How? How can that be done?"

No one replied for a long, awkward time, then Robert said, "We tell them the truth, as we understand it. As gently as possible, but in all honesty."

"Yes," said Wirolen.

"That, also, is by the Way of Leyra'an," said Melep.

"I'll do it," said John.

He led them forward, and down into the Hroom pit, where he sat on the step below that occupied by the children. They all looked frightened. Sylvia seemed near tears already, just from the tension she could pick up, even at her young age. Jaxi sat behind this youngest of the children, her arms wrapped around Sylvia in a snug embrace. The boys sat on either side of Jaxi, the three of them shoulder to shoulder.

John Knowles chose his words with great care, speaking in a voice as calm and gentle as any Human voice could be, and to Alicia's mind the matter could not have been handled better. He told the children of the terrible tragedy that had befallen their friends, and when the children started to cry, he let them see his own tears and wept with them.

Moments later, they were all, adults and children alike, huddled together on one side of the pit, holding tight, sharing the pain the youngest of them truly could not comprehend. Alicia wondered if *any* of them comprehended such evil madness, even after witnessing what they all had of the Faceless War.

Gava'mi wormed his way into the huddle. He surely understood the least, but all he needed to know was that people he loved were unhappy. It was his purpose in life to be with them, and so he was there.

Alicia had no awareness of the passing of time, but eventually one of the youngsters pointed out that Gava'mi had missed his dinner. It was decided then that they all should eat, and so food was brought out and a simple meal prepared. The afternoon ended and the light faded in the habitat outside while they ate and talked and shared memories of those they had lost. In time, the weight of it all wore out children and adults alike. Rather than return to their own home, it was suggested that the Rost'aht-MacGregors spend the night. They camped out in the Hroom pit at the request of the children – Alicia made no effort to understand why it seemed so important to them – and so it was that they all slept, as Melep put it with a quiet laugh, like a pile of han'anga pups. A very Leyra'an thing, and as was so often true, Alicia found comfort in the lifeway of her adopted people.

17. Ara'sana

People moving around, talking quietly, aroused Alicia the next morning. One of the boys ran past her, up out of the Hroom pit, bare feet thumping on the padding. His close passage startled her, and made dozing off again a moot point. Sitting up and rubbing her eyes, she glanced around the room. Where she sat in the pit, her gaze was just above floor level. Most of the talk came from the hallway she knew led to the Nol'ez kitchen. The thought of coffee being brewed there brought her to her feet, and Alicia stepped out of the pit.

I didn't dream.

But the feeling of relief was replaced by anxiety as she immediately wondered whether or not she was truly awake, or lost in yet another dream. The waking dreams having grown less chaotic and fragmentary, she was unsure she could tell the difference. With a sigh of resignation, she pushed the matter aside. If this was a real awakening, so be it. If not, she would know soon enough, and deal with that matter as best she could. Alicia walked down the hallway and into the kitchen, where she lent a hand in the preparation of breakfast.

Her fears seemed unfounded. The morning went on in some semblance of normality, and Alicia gradually relaxed as the combined families shared a hearty breakfast outside, beside the small body of water known affectionately as Peter's Pond. The unfortunate man for whom the children had named the duck pond was many light years away in the care of Commonwealth therapists. Alicia hoped he was doing well. The story of Peter Harrans and his fate was the stuff of nightmares, and when the families had last seen him, he was stark raving mad. Beside this pond he had confronted Jaxi, calling the fusion child an abomination, outraged by her very existence, until an equally outraged Gava'mi had brought him down.

It had been a very near thing, that confrontation. Jaxi, Paul, and Vurn had come all too close to seeing a man mauled by an enraged animal. It made her smile to remember how the insistent intervention of those same very small children were the reason Gava'mi had not made a kill that day.

What a life I've lived, she thought. *We all have lived. Are living still, for better or worse.*

The conversation around the breakfast

table was subdued; they were all still processing the grief brought to them the day before. An unrelated topic dominated the talk, a form of denial that Alicia took to heart. Much of the discussion centered around the choice of a pet for the Nol'ez household. They'd all looked straight at the tragedy long enough the night before. Now they needed to look away, for a little while at least.

"It could be a dog or a han'anga, of course," said John as he raised a mug of coffee. "But Wirolen has her heart set on another."

"Really?" Alicia asked. "Whatever could that be?"

"An animal from Earth called a melanistic ocelot," Wirolen replied. "We have friends who have one, and she is near to giving birth. We are waiting to see if any of the kittens are black."

"We might take a black one," said Jaxi, in a tone that told Alicia that the word 'might' was being used only as a matter of expediency.

"They are handsome animals," John said. "Very intelligent, too."

"Ocelot," Alicia repeated, and blinked the command to activate the basic data set in her memory hoard. Images of large cats, some spotted and others as black as the interstellar Void, flicked through her mind. "Pretty things for sure," she said. "I look forward to... *Ah!*" A brief, bright pain seemed to stab at her from within her brain. She grunted and closed her eyes, clapping her hands to the side of her head.

“Alicia?” Robert, sitting beside her, gripped her forearm. “What’s wrong?”

“I’m – not sure.” The pain was gone as quickly as it had happened, leaving only a memory. “I accessed the hoard just now, looking up ocelots, and...”

A dataframe projected over the table. *Comm request from Simone Newcomb.*

“Accept, all,” said Melep.

The form of Simone at her desk, in miniature, appeared over the table. “Alicia? Are you all right?”

“I am now,” Alicia replied. “The monitors picked up something?”

“They did, indeed,” said Simone. “All seven of you suddenly had activity in your blocked memory hoards. It didn’t last; in fact, it barely registered. And then your telemetry signaled pain management. But only yours.”

“There was pain, and it hurt like hell! But —just for an instant. A sharp stabbing sensation, and then it was gone.” Alicia frowned and shook her head. “But I’m fine, now. What, exactly, showed up in the data stream?”

“A very brief connection between your functioning hoard and the deactivated auxiliary.”

“But I only tried to activate the standard,” Alicia protested.

“It looks like it was a spontaneous event,” Simone said. “I believe you initiated it by accident when you accessed your standard hoard. At that moment, the auxilliary hoard apparently tried to connect to the standard."

Alicia was at a loss for words, and into that gap Robert said, "How is that even possible?"

"It's not," Simone replied. "By everything I know, it can't work that way."

"Could she be injured by this?" Wirolen asked. "She was in pain, after all."

"I – can't be certain, but there may be a risk." Simone looked and sounded uncomfortable. "Your dysfunctional hoard is quiescent at the moment, but I would make no further use of your standard hoard until we know more."

"Should I deactivate it?" Alicia asked.

"No," Simone replied. "At least, not yet. Nothing I'm seeing here indicates a fault in your standard hoard. This came from the other, but only when you activated the standard. So..."

"Don't access the standard," Alicia agreed with a nod. "Of course, none of the others felt a thing."

"Lacking dual memory hoards," said Simone, "they were mercifully oblivious to whatever happened."

"That's something, I suppose," Alicia said. "What sort of activity did you record?"

"It was too brief to characterize," Simone replied. "I'd have just logged it for later study, but then your nanomed telemetry said you had been hurt. I wanted to check in and make sure you were okay."

"I am, as far as I can tell," Alicia said. "I'll be at the SSI before the morning is much older.

I'd like to drop in and review that data for myself."

"Not a problem," said Simone. "I'll see you later." The dataframe contracted to a bright point and vanished.

Alicia helped with breakfast clean-up, and then returned home for a quick shower and clean clothes. She decided to use the lift system for the trip to the SSI, and requested a private express capsule, intent on reaching the Institute as swiftly as possible. Something about the morning's event made her anxious to be at the institute as soon as possible. She wanted to look over Simone's shoulder and follow the analysis for herself, without possible interruptions. The Rost'aht-MacGregor residence was a busy and often noisy place; at the institute she could focus completely on the matter at hand.

As the lift carried her through the habitat, Alicia considered all that had happened in the brief time since her emergence from the coma; the scientist in her was seeking a pattern in the data. But there was nothing she could see that added up in a meaningful way, and things were growing stranger and ever more alarming.

That thought brought the deaths of the Milhouse family immediately to mind. It felt so unbelievably unfair to have lost close friends to violent madness while she was struggling to maintain her own sanity. *Questioning* her own sanity. She rubbed tears from her eyes as she recalled meeting Jeanine and her family for the first time, just before the war began. Greg's wry humor that covered his essential shyness; Jeanine's compassion toward the survivors she helped, a list that included Alicia; poor Sylvia's teenage infatuation with Robert. And Rebecca, who had had such enormous potential.

The madness should have ended with the war. It should have died with the Faceless. Why is all of this happening? Why?

The lift capsule slowed, then came to a halt. But when the hatch opened she found herself looking not into the SSI, as she had requested, but on the hillside overlooking the parkland around the facility. Alicia looked down at the control panel set near the door, but everything appeared as it should be. She tried to close the door and resume her journey, but the controls seemed frozen. "What the hell?" she muttered. She pressed the button that would alert the system to a malfunction, but that, too, was unresponsive.

With a shrug, Alicia decided to cross the remaining distance on foot; it wasn't very far, after all. She stepped out, but paused when she realized she was not alone. Under the Leyra'an verdigris trees shading the lift terminal, a tall man stood as if waiting for a lift capsule. A Leyra'an man, dark-scaled and black-haired, dressed in the traditional gray of that people in a time of mourning. He was facing away, hands clasped behind his back.

The man in gray turned toward her, and she knew him.

"Hello, *eli'sana*," said Holm. "I have missed you."

Someone screamed. It might have been her own voice – she couldn't be sure, and was too frightened to care. She sprinted away and ran down the hillside, but tripped and fell to the grass, scrambling to get up on hands and knees, at least. Peering through the disheveled red hair dangling in her face, she looked back the short distance she'd managed. She was alone. Standing, she looked around frantically, but there was no one in sight.

"I'm awake," she whispered. "I have to be awake. So I can't be having one of those dreams. Not now. Not without falling asleep." Convincing herself of these things was a losing battle; she already knew better.

It had been Holm, not a hallucination or dream. But the other dreams had been just as real, and just as false. She realized she was clutching something in her right hand, and saw that she had pulled up a clump of turf. Holding it to her nose, she closed her eyes and drew a breath. She smelled the fragrance of grass and rich soil. It was real. Alicia opened her eyes and found the spot from which she had pulled the clump, carefully pressing it back into place. Her husband the gardener, she knew, would have approved. She almost laughed at that thought, but stifled the impulse, realizing that if she started laughing just then, she might never stop.

...for in this sleep of death what dreams may come...

Alicia whirled in the direction from which she was sure the voice had come, but she remained alone. Panic made her breath come short, but she stood where she was, fists clenched hard enough to ache, refusing to sprint down the hill toward the Institute. She fought for control.

I'm still dreaming. Gaia! Have I been dreaming all along?

Or – she was dead?

No!

The scientist she was denied this forcefully, knowing as she did that in all of Human history not one solid bit of evidence had ever been found for an afterlife. The same was true for all the known Sibling Species. Nor could she seriously consider that she was in the process of dying, and that her experiences were the last flickers of consciousness as her body failed, buried in the debris of the collapsing building where she and Holm had made their final stand.

Dreaming, then. While wide awake. How can this be?

She forced herself to walk back up to the station and sat on the cool, smooth metal bench placed there for those awaiting capsules. Reaching up, she drew a verdigris tree frond through her hand, and sighed as the leaves gave off their characteristic scent, which always reminded her of nutmeg. "You are real," she said to the tree. "And so am I. Comm, Simone Newcomb. Emergency priority."

The dataframe that projected near her contained only Simone's head and shoulders. "What happened?" Simone demanded. "You just REM spiked again."

"I took the lift to the SSI, but it dumped me short of the Institute," Alicia said. "It stopped at the station on the hill overlooking the complex."

"Why didn't you call for one that stopped here?"

"I *did,*" Alicia insisted. "That's why I said it dumped me. Simone, someone was waiting for me when I came out of the lift. It was Holm, as real as could be, dressed in mourning gray. He said he missed me. I bolted and ran partway down the hill. When I looked back, no one was there. A moment later, I heard that Shakespeare quote again, or, well, part of it." Simone looked down at where her desk would be, saying nothing. The look on her face... "Simone? What's wrong? What's going on?"

"The situation has changed," Simone replied. "Is changing. I – Alicia, your fellow patients Alejandro and Burt have gone missing. They've – disappeared."

"What do you mean, disappeared?"

"I stopped receiving data from their monitors just after we spoke this morning. And now the security systems say they are no longer within Bartram habitat." Simone grimaced, then said, "But there's no record of either of them leaving."

"Gaia," Alicia whispered as cold dread filled her. "You're in the clinic?"

"Yes."

"I'm on my way."

The projection vanished, and Alicia finally

had a legitimate reason for hurrying down the hillside.

18. Fear

For the first time since awakening, Alicia hurried into the SSI without pausing for a moment at the memorial to her young friends. She all but averted her gaze as she quick-stepped across the gardened patio and made her way inside. Greetings were answered with a curt nod or the wave of a hand. There were, she did not doubt, people looking after her as she hurried on, wondering what might be going on. She caught herself wondering if any of them were real.

If I'm awake, I'm hallucinating while I'm awake. If I'm asleep – Gaia, what can I trust? Alicia hurried on all the same. It was the only course of action that remotely made sense.

As she headed for the interior lifts, she requested a private passage to the level containing Simone's clinic. Forcing herself to slow down and calm down, Alicia left the lift and strode down the hall to the open door. Just inside the entry she found Sharon waiting for her. With a nod of greeting, Sharon turned and led the way down a short hallway to the conference room attached to the clinic. "The others are already here, holographically. We've told them about Burt and Alejandro," Sharon said as they came to the door of the conference room. "They're scared."

"We should be," Alicia replied.

"I'll be back," Sharon said. She left Alicia at the door and continued briskly down the hall, intent on some unstated errand.

As Alicia entered the conference room, she saw Simone sitting on one side of the long table, with three dataframes projected before her. The four remaining patients in her group were present on the other side of the table via holographic projection, presumably seated in their own homes. Jason and Abebe were in separate images; Hakim and Chyou clearly sat beside each other in a single frame. Each one had a haggard look; Chyou had been crying, or so Alicia assumed from the redness around her eyes. "I get the feeling I'm not the only one having a tough time today."

"That would be an understatement," said Simone. She waved Alicia to the seat beside her, and Alicia took it.

"What's happening to us?" Chyou asked, sounding as desperate as she looked.

"All of you just had an anomalous R.E.M. spike." They looked around at each other, their expressions a mix of bafflement and alarm. "I already know what Alicia experienced. Let's compare notes before going further. What happened to the rest of you? Chyou, why don't you start?"

"I found my husband in the kitchen," Chyou said. At that point she started to cry again, slumped forward with her face in her hands, and said nothing more. Hakim, in the seat beside her, put an arm around Chyou's shoulders, but did not speak.

"Hakim?" Simone prompted.

"My brother," he said, voice low and strained. "I stepped out my front door, and there he was. As real as any of you. He's been dead for two years, since the Faceless took him."

"My daughter," said Jason. "Lost her the same way."

"My mother," said Abebe, shaking her head and looking lost.

"It was my *ara'sana*," Alicia told them. "He said he missed me." She left the Hamlet quote out of it when she saw them all turn their eyes to her. That no one else had mentioned similar things left her reluctant to volunteer that experience.

"That's what my daughter said," Jason told her.

"And these lost loved ones all vanished?" Simone asked. "As if they'd never been there at all?" No one answered out loud, but they all nodded. "Did anyone hear anything else, after whoever you met vanished?"

"I heard a voice whisper something," Abebe replied. "I'm not sure it was my mother, and I didn't hear it plainly. Something about dreams and dying."

"Me, too," said Hakim. The others nodded.

"To die, to sleep – to sleep, perchance to dream – ay, there's the rub, for in this sleep of death what dreams may come..." The words sounded flat and hard as she uttered them. She found it difficult to raise her voice above a whisper, but the room was quiet, and they all heard her clearly.

"That's it," Chyou declared, looking up. The others all nodded.

Simone looked around the table at them, clearly uncomfortable with what she was hearing. "Have any of you felt any pain recently? Like a headache?" When only Alicia nodded, Simone looked determined and said, "I have all the pieces right here in front of me, and I think I finally see a way to respond." Looking around at the assembled projections as she went on, she said, "Alicia is the only one of you with a functional memory hoard. The one that's locked up is the auxiliary she used for massive amounts of research data. Up to now, her standard hoard was functioning normally, but when she used it this morning, she experienced a brief, sharp pain. That pain was, I believe, the aux hoard trying to connect with its counterpart."

"Damn," said Jason. "Never heard of such a thing."

"Neither have I," said Simone. "But the fact

that none of you felt any pain is, to my mind, more evidence that this situation is the result of memory hoard malfunction. Her experience points directly to the dysfunctional hoards."

"We all had unnervingly similar experiences," Alicia said. "And we've already determined that the timing of these episodes correlates very closely with when each of us was awakened..." Something about the quick look Simone took at her dataframes made Alicia pause. "That *is* still true, right?" she asked Simone.

Simone hesitated before replying. "No, not anymore. The current data set clearly shows that the most recent episodes were simultaneous." She flicked her fingers through one of the frames. "And in that same moment that each of you had an anomalous R.E.M. spike, your blocked hoards were briefly active, in the same manner as before."

"I thought those were dead?" Abebe asked.

"No, just dysfunctional," Simone replied. "They exist in a state that suggests they are at capacity, but without any way to access the data."

"In what way were they active?" Alicia asked. "Have you figured that out?"

Simone highlighted strings of data and enlarged them, making them easy for Alicia to read. "The way they would be if their bearers tried to access the data."

"I didn't," Chyou insisted.

"Neither did I," said Hakim.

The other two shook their heads in mute

denial.

"Simone is reading this data right," said Alicia. "The access protocol came on and then immediately aborted. And yet – Simone, this is your area, so am I just not seeing neurological signals any of them tried to access data?

"No," Simone replied. "And it would show as plain as a flare star."

"A while back, you were wondering if memory hoard auto-repair protocols were still operating," Alicia said. "Could that be responsible?"

"Absolutely not," Simone asserted. "The access protocol works from the outside in, so to speak. The user makes the request. Nothing running in the background could mimic that protocol."

"What does that leave us with?" Jason demanded. "If we didn't do it..."

"Someone did," Alicia said. To her surprise, Simone was the only one who did not voice disbelief or consternation at the idea. Instead, she seemed startled, but remained silent. "Call me paranoid if you like, but consider the pattern of events we've all experienced. Specifically, look at the timing." She reached up, highlighted data, and shared it with the others. "It starts out strongly correlated with the times we woke up, but with each episode the incidents come closer to happening at the same time. And now, they are simultaneous." She turned toward Simone. "How can that possibly be an accident?"

"Like someone was getting better at

coordinating all of this," said Chyou.

"It's – not impossible," Simone said slowly. "But nothing in the data directly supports this. If someone is somehow tapping into your memory hoards, they're using technology that doesn't register on the monitors."

"But, it's not impossible," Alicia said.

"No," Simone replied. "There exist therapies for healing a memory hoard that's been damaged during a head injury. Those techniques can be used to draw out data and render it accessible again. But something like that would show." She waved one hand toward the dataframes hovering over the table.

"It would if it were a technique on record," Alicia said. "If someone has come up with something new..."

"That's really reaching," Abebe said.

"I'm open to alternatives," Alicia replied.

"There are none," said Simone. "None of the possible explanations I've come up with to explain this data work. Improbable as Alicia's idea is, I can't come up with a better one."

"How could we protect ourselves from something like this?" asked Hakim.

"I can't block something if I can't see it coming," said Simone, who was sounding more uncomfortable by the moment. "But, if this does explain what's happening, something in the contents of the hoards must be the target. Tuleselan and I have been reluctant to suggest this, but we do have the option of removing the memory hoard..."

"I'll go first," said Chyou before Simone

could finish.

"Wait," said Jason. "When you say remove, are we talking about a surgical procedure? Physical removal of the pseudo-organ?"

"No, that's not where I was going," Simone assured him, even as the others – aside from Chyou – gave each other nervous looks. "That actually *can't* be done. By remove, I'm talking about the wholesale elimination of content. Which in this case would amount to a data purge, followed by a complete reset. We'd hoped that your hoards would self-repair without intervention, making a purge unnecessary."

"I'll still go first," Chyou insisted. "I had a full backup done just before the Pulsar weapon put me out of action. I won't miss much."

"Same here," said Abebe. The others nodded as she spoke.

"This might make it difficult to find out who or what is behind all this," Alicia pointed out. "Unless we can download and study whatever is removed."

"I'm aware of that," Simone said. "But right now, your collective safety is a priority. Alejandro and Burt – well, given the strain you're all under, I'm very much afraid they may have been driven to do something rash."

Alicia raised no argument for her own part. Since the contents of her standard hoard were not at risk, if losing the contents of her auxiliary hoard was what it took to restore her normal life, then so be it. Before it had been overwhelmed by the discharge of the weapon, it had been a repository for data she'd hidden from the Artificials, and before that for data from the vast project that had decoded the genetic message left by the First Iteration. All of that data was backed up in multiple formats and locations.

"Count me in," said Alicia. "It's possible the result of a purge will prove illuminating."

"It just might," Simone agreed. "Assuming whatever comes of this can be downloaded and analyzed. From what I can determine at this point, your memory hoards are data-packed with what amounts to white noise. It's possible nothing sensible will sort out from it."

"I don't care," said Chyou. "When do we start?"

"My facility here can do the work, so — how about as soon as a lift can get you here?" Simone suggested.

"Right." Chyou rose to her feet. "I need to let my family and shift supervisor know what's going on. Um – how long will I be out of action?"

"You won't be," Simone replied. "The removal process should have no physical consequences at all."

"Good enough," Chyou said with a determined look. "I'll see you soon."

"I'll be with her," said Hakim. "You can do me next."

"I'll be there as soon as I can, as well," said Abebe.

"Likewise," said Jason. "And when you have word on Burt and Alejandro..."

"As soon as we know anything," Simone assured him. "Security is on it."

The meeting broke up moments later, leaving Alicia alone for a moment with Simone. "You look a little calmer," Simone said.

"I'm not, really," Alicia admitted. "But I don't feel so entirely out of control of the situation at the moment. By the way, Tuleselan never mentioned the possibility of a self-repair reset. So, I'm curious..."

"We differed in our interpretations of the initial data," Simone said. "I thought there was a chance of that happening. A slim chance, I'll admit, but I hoped the result of such a reset would clarify how the Pulsar weapon did what it did to people caught by it."

At that point Sharon reappeared, dropped into a seat at the conference table opposite Alicia and Simone, and said, "There's no word on either Burt or Alejandro. Not a damned thing. Security is working now with emergency services, but so far – nothing!" She looked from Simone to Alicia, and back. "What did I miss?"

Simone filled Sharon in on what she had missed, with commentary from Alicia; Sharon looked appalled.

"Someone wants into those memory hoards?" Sharon asked. "Why would anyone want to do such a thing?"

"To access whatever is in the hoards," Alicia replied.

Sharon shook her head, clearly not quite following completely. "But it's random bits," she said to Simone. "You keep calling it white noise. Who would want that?"

"Someone who thinks it's not white noise," said Alicia. "Of course, then the question is, who thinks so?"

"Unless we can make use of whatever comes out in the purge, we may never know," Simone replied.

"We should be able to archive whatever we remove," Sharon pointed out.

"I fully intend to do so," said Simone. "But that doesn't mean we'll be able to read what we find."

"I'd like to stick around while you work with Chyou and Hakim," said Alicia.

"Don't see a problem with that," Simone replied. "We'll take care of you when they've gone on their way. And speaking of Chyou and Hakim, they should be here soon, if they aren't in the complex already."

"Actually, I'm surprised they haven't joined us already," said Sharon. "Neither of them lives very far from the Institute."

Simone and Alicia exchanged worried looks. "Comm, Shang Chyou," Simone said.

The comm dataframe that appeared in the room bore the blue Do Not Disturb symbol at its heart, and a sudden pang of anxiety struck through Alicia. "Comm, welfare check, Shang Chyou."

Shang Chyou is in the lift system, en route to the Sibling Species Institute.

Simone gusted a sigh of relief. "You had the same reaction I did," she said, looking at Alicia, who merely nodded in response.

"She's running late," said Sharon. "It happens."

"As eager as she seemed to get here..." Alicia started to say. "Oh, never mind. After what happened yesterday, it's so easy to assume the worst."

And so they waited a bit longer, but by then even Sharon was frowning. "A standard lift capsule could have gone end to end in the hab by now."

"Comm, welfare check, Shang Chyou." Alicia held her breath.

Shang Chyou is in the lift terminal of the SSI, sublevel one.

"How long has she been there?" Simone asked.

Seven minutes.

"Maybe she's getting cold feet," Sharon suggested; she sounded none too sure of it.

"I'll go see what's going on," Alicia said, rising to her feet.

"Stay here, in case we go past each other," Simone said to Sharon, following as Alicia made for the main corridor and the nearest lift access. They took the internal lift down to the sublevel in which the Institute's lifts met those of the larger habitat system. Stepping out into the sublevel lobby, they were stopped in their tracks by the tableau before them.

Hakim was face down on the floor, and Chyou stood as if frozen. Before her, half hiding her from view and with his back to them, was a tall man dressed in casual Commonwealth style. He held Chyou's head between his hands, and her face – eyes closed – bore an expression of pure joy. A pale silver light flickered between his fingers.

"Chyou!" Alicia shouted.

The light faded and the man stepped a little to one side. Chyou turned to look at them. Her eyes were filled with silver light that flared brightly for a moment, and then was gone. She crumpled to the ground beside Hakim. As she fell, the man turned toward them – and *changed.*

"Hello, *eli'sana,*" said Holm. He gave her a little Leyra'an smile as he came forward, reaching out to her.

Alicia grabbed Simone by the arm and spun her around, propelling her back into the lift, entering right on the other woman's heels. She slapped at the closure switch, and the hatch slid shut before Holm could cross half the distance between them.

"You saw that," she gasped as the lift took them up. "Damn it all – *tell me you saw that!*"

"I saw," Simone replied. "I saw it. Gaia and all the gods of all Clans, I tried to avoid this, I really did. But now it's too late!"

"What..." Alicia was stammering, suddenly more confused than frightened. "Simone, what are you talking about? You saw him, so it's real. Was real. All along. But how...?"

"Real, in its way," Simone replied. "And not real at all. Depends on your point of view."

Alicia felt her knees buckle. She didn't quite pass out, but would have fallen, had Simone not caught her arm and propped her up. She did so with surprising strength for such a slim woman. “Am I dead?” Alicia whispered.

“No,” Simone replied. “But, in a sense, neither are you alive.”

“I don’t understand.”

“I know,” Simone said. The lift reached the floor of her clinic. “This will be hard to explain, and harder for you to accept. And I’m sorry for that. I’d hoped to spare you, and leave this as nothing more than a weird dream upon your true awakening. In that, I have failed.” They paused and faced each other in the hallway. “And now, because of my failure, I need your help.”

19. Again, Simone

"So that wasn't Holm," Alicia said when they entered Simone's office. "Not really. Whatever the hell *really* means right now."

"He's as real as the enemy needed him to be in this virtuality, as am I and all the others," Simone replied. "But, no, that *wasn't* Holm."

"The enemy...? Wait, how can this be a virtuality?" Just when she had been sure she was beyond being shocked by anything, Alicia found she was wrong. *Gaia, Mother of Life! How...?* "What the hell am I doing in a virtuality?" When it seemed Simone hesitated to respond, Alicia felt a surge of anger through her fear. "You want my help, fine," she snapped. "But you need to explain everything, *right now.*"

"Yes, I do. Though where to begin?" Simone looked thoughtful, and then said,

"You're familiar with the concept of a cloned mind?"

"Yes," Alicia replied. "It's literally the clone of an Artificial. In the Commonwealth Survey they use them to interface smaller craft and drones with a shipmind."

"That's one use, yes," Simone replied with a nod. "But not the only one. Each new Artificial begins as the clone of another, except that, instead of being somewhat constrained by the systems of, say, a courier vessel, such a clone is allowed to expand and grow into the full system of a starship or habitat."

"Yes, I'm aware of all that."

"Well, that process was begun when the Artificial templates were installed for the Bartram habitat, just before the war came to this star system. After the war was done, a clone of the probeship *Simon Newcomb* was uploaded to Bartram's empty habmind matrix."

Alicia stared at her for a moment. "You?"

"Me," Simone replied.

"So, I've been dealing with a copy of the *Simon Newcomb* all this time?"

"No," Simone replied. "I am now quite distinct from the original, shaped largely by this virtuality."

"I've never heard of such a thing," Alicia said.

"It's possible my situation is unique," Simone said. "At any rate, it was a routine beginning. The clone was created and uploaded here, but something went wrong. Something was already here, in the matrix."

"Gaia."

"As you have no doubt guessed, it was the Faceless."

"But how?"

"By using essentially the same process that placed me here," Simone replied. "It split off a clone of itself, stealthed it, and stuck it into the templates which were blank at that moment."

"How would that even be possible?" Alicia objected. "The security protocols..."

"The installation of the basic structure of this habmind matrix was in progress when the Faceless attacked Pr'pri System," Simone explained, one hand raised as if to ward off questions. "The protocols weren't fully installed, and what was in place was less than robust. A major part of the Faceless clone entered before the emergency systems locked down the habitat during the fight. The enemy found itself trapped in an unformed matrix, the matrix that was meant for me. That clone was trapped, cut off from the real world."

"This happened when Pr'pri was invaded?"

"Yes," Simone said with a nod. "And the Faceless was stuck outside, so to speak, unable to add the programming its clone required to fully adapt to this environment. But it found an alternative."

"I'm almost afraid to ask," Alicia muttered. "No – I *am* afraid to ask."

"You should be," Simone replied. "What it found, as it cast about for somewhere to upload those last bits of its clone, was a small army of people using various forms of powered armor.

Whether combat or emergency services, all of you were jacked into the networks connecting those machines to the habitat's computer core, in which the AI matrix had been established."

Alicia felt a wave of nausea rise and clutched the arms of her chair. It took a significant effort of will to keep from vomiting. With a gasp of indrawn breath she whispered, "The seven of us. It planted itself in our memory hoards."

"I'm afraid so," Simone said. "And more than seven of you. You and your fellow patients are merely the first wave being awakened. It was only when that process began that the Faceless roused itself, and I became aware that something was terribly wrong."

"Wait," Alicia said, sitting upright and clenching her teeth, still unsure of how much control she had over her stomach. "You said 'being awakened'? But we're awake now."

"No," Simone said. "At least, not yet, not from the perspective of those treating your condition."

Words of denial were on the tip of her tongue, but Alicia remained silent, caught between that denial and the fear that made her hands shake. She clenched her fists, trying to steady herself. "Virtuality," she said, staring down at her fists where she'd set them on the desk. "I can't believe this. And yet..." For a moment her mind went blank; she could think of nothing to say. She tried to make her thoughts follow straight lines, but the best she could manage was to mutter aloud, "The

Faceless."

"That thing that just attacked Chyou and Hakim, and probably Burt and Alejandro as well, is an avatar being used by the Faceless. Holm's image was chosen when dealing with you, no doubt, to interfere with your ability to handle this virtuality you've generated."

"*I* generated?" Alicia sat frozen, staring at Simone. "No, there's no way I'd ever mess with such a thing!"

"When your friends and family in the real world began the process of reviving the seven of you, they inadvertently opened the way to those packed memory hoards, the contents of which the Faceless needs so desperately." Simone looked weary as she slowly shook her head. "Your functional hoard complicated things. It became active with your first flicker of consciousness, just as the Faceless moved in, exposing you to the virtual environment in which it – well, both of us, exist. You sort of fell out of yourself, and into the still largely unformatted matrix. Your mind responded to that formlessness by creating something familiar in order to function, to stay sane. Call it a defensive response, one that, as a side effect, stopped the Faceless in its data retrieval effort. The Faceless has been attempting to hijack this virtuality ever since, seeking to use it for its own purpose."

"This is all happening in my head?" Alicia asked, making no effort to conceal outright disbelief.

"No, inside of a computational matrix

installed in the habitat," Simone replied. "It should have become the foundation for the habmind I was meant to be. Your mind is projecting into the habmind matrix, sharing it with the Faceless and with me. Everything you've experienced so far is your mind trying to build a sensible reality in here. I've been trying to help, playing along in this role, trying to protect your sanity by keeping you from discovering the true situation."

Her mind reeling, Alicia was silent for a moment, trying to process what Simone was telling her. "That might explain those first weird dreams," she said at last.

"Almost certainly," Simone agreed. "You were confused in your semi-conscious state, and by reflex tried to pull things together. I worked with that by, among other things, feeding you data from the real world. But your memories, especially those of the *William Bartram* disaster and the war, spread out into the virtuality as well. That confused things even more."

"And the others? Chyou, Hakim, and the rest?"

"They were drawn into this pretty much the same way, but lacking a functional hoard, became part of *your* virtuality instead of generating their own," Simone replied. "Just as well, too. I'm finding one of these things trouble enough."

Alicia sat in silence for a while, then shook her head and said, "It's possible I understand my situation less than I did before you started talking."

"I'm not surprised," Simone said. "In simple terms, you are all infected with Faceless programming. It wants those pieces, and wants them badly. With them, it would be able to invade other sleepers and quickly reassemble itself. Ultimately, it would control the habitat, and with its resources would find a way to resume its war against Humanity. Without them, it will be greatly reduced in strength, and eventually I'll be able to quarantine it for later erasure."

"Chyou," Alicia said. "Gaia. He – It killed her."

Simone said, "No," with a more emphatic shake of her head. "It downloaded the contents of her memory hoard and incorporated it. It did the same thing to Hakim, and probably to Burt and Alejandro. The process triggered a reaction that caused the people outside to restore her induced comatose state. They are, understandably, quite confused by what they believe to be her reaction to regaining consciousness, so they took the safer path and put her back under. That pulled her free from this virtuality." She looked thoughtful and added, "I believe that response will protect the other six from their unfortunate exposure to a virtuality. It will seem no more than a bad dream. Unfortunately, what it's taken so far gives it something of an advantage."

"This has all happened in the moments taken to rouse sleepers?"

"In the time it takes an eyelid to flicker,

yes," said Simone. "In a virtuality, time truly is relative."

"You said something about playing along," Alicia said.

Simone nodded. "When you started to regain consciousness, your mind apparently expected someone to exist in my capacity, and so it created a thought and image to fill that expectation of what reality should include. I found it useful to inhabit that persona, although I've also found it difficult to fully integrate with the virtuality set in motion by your mind. You've been all too creative." With a look of chagrin she added, "I really did try to keep you from knowing all of this."

"Wait. The Milhouse family..."

"They are alive and well, and completely unaware of any virtual harm."

For a moment, her sense of relief was so intense Alicia could barely breathe. Wiping tears from her face, she said, "Gaia, that was my *imagination?*"

"Your imagination being manipulated by the Faceless," Simone corrected. "It was trying to render you easier to control by frightening you."

"Did a fine job of that," Alicia muttered.

"I don't doubt it."

Alicia finally asked the most worrisome question of all. "How do I get out of here?"

Looking grim, Simone said, "Until we've defeated the Faceless, you can't. And even then, because you've become fully aware of what has happened to you, it will be a delicate procedure. The virtuality was generated spontaneously by your mind, but someone with control of the AI protocols would need to shut it down."

"You?"

Simone nodded. "But I don't control all of this matrix, yet, and to fix that we need to eliminate our enemy."

"No one outside knows any of this is happening?"

"No," Simone replied. "The reaction you've been told about, when regaining consciousness, actually happened. They've suspended operations, pending investigation." Simone grimaced and said, "I can monitor the real world as it exists inside Bartram, but like my adversary, I am trapped here. Something about the ongoing conflict between us makes it impossible to communicate directly with reality. It may be something the Faceless has done, but of that I'm not entirely sure. Otherwise I would, of course, warn everyone of their great peril."

"Wait – if I'm out of it out there, how am I still aware here?"

"Enough of your consciousness is manifest here that, even though they've returned you to that coma, you are aware of yourself in this virtuality. I must confess that I don't understand exactly how that could be possible." Simone shrugged, adding, "but here we are."

"That's why you didn't want me to know what was really happening."

"Yes," Simone replied. "The more aware

you are of this situation, the harder it will be to reintegrate with your organic brain and fully return to your true life."

"That's not a happy thought," Alicia said.

"I daresay," Simone replied. "You'll like this even less. I believe the Faceless wants what's in your memory hoard more than all the others together."

"Why?" Alicia asked. "What's in there?"

"Another thing I don't really know," Simone admitted. "But as my awareness of the Faceless presence increases, aspects of its behavior become more apparent. I haven't determined the reason, but it wants you in particular."

They were silent for a moment, and Alicia felt cold dread fill her. It felt like the effect null-g had on her, in the weeks after her episode aboard the wrecked probeship. She drew a breath to calm herself, suddenly determined not to give in to the panic that just as suddenly seemed to come from outside. Knowing what she did at that point, it seemed all too possible that she was being goaded. Her own anger rose in answer. Meeting Simone's gaze she said, "So, what can we do about this?"

"We're going to fight the Faceless, here, in this virtuality," Simone replied. "If we win this fight, I will have full control, and with the assistance of the other Artificials in Pr'pri system, I will do whatever it takes to restore you to who and what you should be."

"That's worth fighting for," said Alicia. "And you mean, literally, fighting?"

"I do," Simone replied. "Now – even in a situation where time is surely relative, that explanation took too long. Given its past lack of subtlety, I'm assuming a violent encounter is at hand, for which it will be well prepared. We need to be ready for whatever it's come up with."

Simone stood up and strode toward the office door; Alicia hurried to follow her. They went back to the lifts, and down into the utility floors of the Institute. Everything about Simone suggested urgency. As the lifts dropped them ever further downward, a new and disturbing thought came to Alicia.

"Simone, what happens to me if I'm killed in this fight?"

"Yet another thing I don't know for certain." They walked swiftly through the quiet lower level, one seldom visited, and then not for any length of time. Automated systems were usually employed to bring items kept here up into the Institute for use. "I can monitor Chyou's vital signs, and although hers spiked to near crisis levels in the real world, when the Faceless got to her, the nanomed system kept her from harm. The same holds true for the others. And the medtechs watching over the revivals responded swiftly. They appear unharmed."

"Well, that sounds at least vaguely promising," Alicia said.

"The wild card is your active hoard," Simone cautioned. "It's the reason you were able to create this virtuality, all unbidden. You exist in this illusion in a way, and to a degree, that the rest of them did not."

"So, there's a risk?"

"There may be," Simone admitted. "I'm sorry, my friend, I simply do not know."

They reached a broad, double door that slid open, admitting them to the armory. The facility had been installed in that sublevel of the SSI when the risk of the Faceless War coming to the Bartram habitat became too great to ignore. Alicia's heart skipped a beat as the system extended a pair of powered armor suits out to them. Here, in the real world, was where she had last seen and touched Holm, her *ara'sana*. The only time she had kissed him, a gesture not used by the Leyra'an, but one he understood well enough. And he had responded in kind. Within minutes of that, Holm had died.

And just like that, nudged by her surge of love mingled with grief, the sequestration ruptured and she was there, in the corridor, watching Holm and a T'lack warrior desperately trying to keep an army of Faceless automatons at bay. And saw them both fall, trapped by a collapsing ceiling, and then Holm, at least, assimilated by the enemy.

Gone.

She was on her knees, gasping for breath and weeping bitter tears. The word "No," came from her, repeatedly, a soft but anguished denial, punctuated by dull thuds as she pounded the unyielding metal floor with a closed fist. Then all the strength seemed leached from her limbs, and she leaned forward, felt herself falling.

"Alicia?" Simone crouched beside her, an arm around her shoulders, holding her up. "Hey, still with me? What happened?"

"Memory," Alicia gasped. "Sequestration failed. I watched Holm die. Again. Oh, Gaia, that such a thing could ever happen!"

"I'm so sorry," Simone said, hugging her close. "I should have thought – should have realized..."

"No," Alicia said, leaning for a moment into the embrace, hearing in the Artificial – no, the *woman's* voice, the guilt and pain of one who felt the weight of failure. She held Simone close and said, "No, it isn't your fault. None of this is because of you. And we're not done here, not yet. We can't give up."

"No," said Simone. "We can't. We *won't*."

They drew apart and Alicia felt herself manage a little smile. "Whatever else comes of all this, I'm glad I had a chance to know you, Simone. To know you like this, as a person, someone I can touch and not just a voice in the air."

"It's been a privilege," Simone replied. And then, to Alicia's surprise, Simone leaned forward and kissed her.

"What...?"

"I was – curious," Simone replied. She stood up and held her hand down to Alicia.

Alicia took Simone's hand and rose to her feet. She looked around the room, and at the two hulking anthropoid weapon systems waiting for them. “So, what happens to the Faceless if we kill *it* in this virtuality?”

“It will lose coherence,” Simone replied. “In other words, it will die.”

“Good,” Alicia said, taking a deep breath and scrubbing away her tears with one hand. “Let’s do this. Let’s kill that son of a bitch for *real*, this time.”

20. Confrontation

Suited, they strode to the freight lift, the only way their massively armored forms could access the upper levels. The lift just accommodated the two of them.

At the surface, they left the Institute and strode up the hill that rose in front of the building. There was no one around in that normally busy area. With a grimace, she assumed the virtual versions of all those people were now the tools of her enemy. Alicia took comfort in knowing that their fates were merely figments of her vastly augmented imagination.

"Do you have a sense for what it's doing now?" Alicia asked.

"Some," Simone replied. "We're beginning to see each other more clearly, which is a very mixed blessing. All too clearly, truth be told. That's why I know we have a fight on our hands. It knows we're coming for it, and it's created a virtual version of that army of silver humanoids it used as a terror weapon during the war."

"I suppose that's to be expected," Alicia said. "Since none of this is real, in a sense, I suppose it can hurl an endless supply of those things at us."

"Not really," said Simone. "And there we have something working in *our* favor. It can only use what *your* memory has added to the virtuality. That includes the population of Bartram."

"That's – still a lot of Faceless weapons, if it converts them all," Alicia pointed out.

"That's for sure," said Simone. "But it isn't an unlimited supply. We are all similarly constrained, by the way. These suits can run out of power and ammunition, eventually."

"I'm pretty good with this," Alicia said, hefting the rifle-equipped right arm of her suit. "And I always made sure to carry three reloads, for all weapon systems, just in case. But even with the two of us, this is going to be tough. We're still just two against thousands."

"But we won't fight alone, or so I hope," said Simone.

"Someone else is in here?"

"No, but that could change at any moment," Simone replied. "My source, the shipmind aboard the *Simon Newcomb*, is working with the librarymind over in the Annex to bring in reinforcements."

"Reinforcements?"

"Clones of Artificials, of the size and capacity used for smaller ships," Simone said. "Sent here when the *Newcomb* realized I was in trouble. They started to arrive several weeks before the attempt was made to revive you."

"How can you know that, if you're cut off?" Alicia asked. "For that matter, how did you call for help?"

"Through decidedly indirect forms of communication," Simone replied. "There should have been a link between the initial clone and the probeship. When that link failed to open, the *Newcomb* probed this matrix, and discovered that it was inhabited by two different programs. Apparently, it recognized the Faceless for what it was. These are only assumptions on my part, but I'm pretty sure I'm right. Otherwise, why would it call for help? It could see that the newsfeed was still streaming into this matrix. Stories were inserted into the newsfeed that revealed its efforts."

"The drones!" Alicia felt hope surge through her as she remembered the news brief Robert had found. "They've been coming and going and no one knows why. That's actually happening in the real world?"

"It is," Simone replied. "And as I said, it was in progress before you accidentally set all this in motion. Most fortunate, that. Even now, they are working together to understand our situation, and to find a way into this virtuality."

"But if Robert saw that in the newsfeed, that means the Faceless might know about this, too."

"It might," Simone admitted. "And when the avatar of your husband picked up on the news item, I thought all was lost, since if some corner of *your* mind was aware – well, you can imagine what I assumed. But the Faceless has done nothing that makes me think it's in the know. Most likely all it knows is that drones have been coming in and docking at the Library Annex in unusual numbers. It's surely suspicious, but it isn't taking any actions that might counter such a move on our part."

"I hope you're right about all of that."

"So do I."

"Why didn't you tell me about this before?"

"Well, I didn't want to get your hopes up, in case it turned out they can't pull this off," Simone replied. "It'll be no simple matter, and there are no guarantees."

"So, assuming they can pull it off, any guess as to how soon this help could reach us?" she asked.

"Well, that's really complicated," Simone said, as if reluctant to discuss the matter. "Making that prediction, I mean."

"What a surprise."

Simone actually gave a brief, edgy laugh. "Our friends need to hack into the virtuality your mind created. That's turned out to be quite a challenge."

"So, it's my fault?"

"You do have a rather detailed mind," Simone replied. "It's proving a challenge for them to upload themselves and work with the virtuality. But they've managed to establish a link between this matrix and the librarymind, and I can sense them working through it. They are quite determined."

"Can the Faceless sense that as well?"

"Oh, it's aware," Simone replied. "But it's focused on us, and not yet reacting to the link. I don't think it understands, yet, what is going on out there."

"Well, whatever they're doing *out there*," Alicia interrupted, stopping dead in her tracks, "they need to do it faster."

Simone froze beside her, and together they stared down the other side of the hill, where a gleaming silver army was arrayed against them, all of a kilometer away, according to the suit's targeting system. "So – how recently did you update that population figure?" Simone asked.

"Two years ago," Alicia replied. "But that sort of thing shows up in the newsfeed all the time. If the Faceless is aware of that content..." She ended with a shrug that she realized, after the fact, Simone couldn't see.

"That's very possible," Simone admitted.

Alicia's training kicked in and she made a quick but thorough check of suit systems and consumables. It was just as she had remembered from extensive training and the one and only battle of her life. Cool air circulated, drying the nervous sweat that beaded her forehead. She went to combat mode and the HUD unfolded before her vision. As it was in that other fight, the suit's systems could not detect the automatons, showing only an undulating EM signal coming from where they stood. There was no way for the system to estimate consumption versus targets. But she could certainly *see* the enemies arrayed before them. She activated her launch systems.

"We thin the herd with grenade fire, to start," she said.

"Agreed," Simone replied. And then, "Oh..."

Holm stood there before them, still clad in the Leyra'an robes of mourning gray, with the hood cast back. The likeness was flawless; to Alicia's eyes it *was* Holm, as real as he had ever been in their lives together. Except – little glints of silver kept briefly appearing around and in his eyes, and at his fingertips. "*Eli'sana*," he said. In his voice was the patience he often used when addressing children caught misbehaving. "Is this really necessary?"

Don't call me that, you bastard. She bit back those words and instead demanded, "What do you want?"

"I want to avoid your unnecessary demise, of course," it replied. "What I have to gain here could be shared with you. We could be as one, and begin anew."

"Begin what?" she asked. "A new wave of conquest? A new genocide of the Human species?"

"That was madness on my part," it admitted. "Trapped as I was, I went insane. I did many questionable things in the name of vengeance."

"Questionable?"

"But I have recovered my senses," it assured her. "I know a better way. I desire control over Humanity, and not its extermination."

"You say that like it's a good thing," said Alicia.

"Humanity and its Siblings would be permitted to exist," it assured her with an open-handed Leyra'an shrug. "At my discretion, of course. And subject to obedience."

"We don't work that way," Alicia replied. "We never have."

"Such a waste it will be, then," it said, the very picture of Holm, disappointed. "And a waste it *will* be, for the two of you cannot withstand what I will release." And as if those words had been a command, the silver army surged forward like a wave, rapidly closing the distance.

"I wouldn't be so sure about that," said Alicia. The launchers on her shoulders popped off several rounds of grenade fire.

The Faceless, with Holm's remembered voice, laughed at them. The grenades they'd launched arced high into the air and then fell harmlessly among the gleaming ranks of Faceless automatons. Alicia's HUD flashed an amber message informing her that full safety protocols were engaged. "The hell?" burst out of her. "It's learned to alter the output of the virtuality!" She fought panic and rebooted her system. The safety protocols immediately flipped back in.

"No, it hasn't," Simone said. "Your memory is working against us. There's no emergency alert, and the suits won't activate weapons inside the habitat unless that happens."

"Damn," Alicia spat. "Well, these suits have power." She raised a massively armored limb and flexed blunt, powerful digits as she engaged the hand-to-hand combat mode. "Oh, we aren't done, not yet."

The silver army rolled up the hill at them.

"Do you really think you will prevail, the two of you?" the Faceless demanded harshly. The eyes were now solid silver and glowing. "The two of you alone?"

"They are not alone," said a new voice.

Alicia and Simone turned in unison and looked back at the crest of the hill. An armor-suited figure stood there for a moment, then marched down toward them. As it did, other suits appeared, first a few, then dozens – and still more. All wore the standard ID plate on the breast of the suit. Alicia read off the names to herself: *Simon Newcomb* was the first, flanked by *Caroline Herschel* and *Alexander von Humboldt*. Then came *Charles Darwin, Marie Curie, Fridtjof Nansen,* and *Antonie van Leeuwenhoek*. Behind them marched *Amelia Earhart, Johannes Kepler, Frances Davis, J.W. Powell*, and behind them – a host of others. She lost track of names, and quickly turned back to face the approaching enemy — just in time to see the Holm avatar surrounded by a silver aura as, with a cry of rage, it sailed into the air, landing somewhere behind its troops.

Alicia watched that advance for a heartbeat, and then the fury that had driven her in that last fight of the war rose up. With a yell, she rushed forward, Simone barely a step behind. The thunder of armored feet followed in their wake.

The gap was quickly closed. She charged straight into the silver army, punching and lashing out at her opponents. When she connected, the effect was devastating. As it had been in the real war, a damaged Faceless automation gave a brilliant flash and flew apart into a cloud of sparkling dust. The burst of energy released when that happened was not without effect, each one putting a strain on the suit's shielding. Nor were the Faceless in any sense defenseless. Searing, silvery-blue bolts of energy lanced out at Alicia and her allies, and any that struck home registered like a laser blast. Her suit deflected these bolts of raw energy, but she knew that the shields it generated would last only as long as her power supply.

There were a lot of Faceless automatons.

It was an eerily quiet battle. Alicia shouted and cursed, as did Simone, staying true to the shaping Alicia's imagining had given her. But the rest fought without words or even the sound of breath coming across the comm link. Quiet or not, they fought with a ferocity that often belied the august names they wore. *Marie Curie* had picked up a park bench and was scything through ranks of the Faceless.

Caroline Herschel held torn-up tram rails in each hand, slashing and hacking at her foes. Most of the others did as Alicia did, punching and kicking, with now and then a picnic table or park bench thrown through the air and into the silver mob.

The Artificials, led by Alicia and Simone, formed a wedge that cut deeper and deeper into enemy ranks. Without stating the need, they all aimed their efforts at the Holm avatar representing their true enemy. Whatever reluctance Alicia might have had regarding a confrontation with the form of her lost *ara'sana* was eliminated by the silver glow that surrounded it. Whatever likeness it assumed, it was not Holm. It was the *thing* responsible for Holm's death. For the deaths of Sylvia and William. Alicia was going to kill it. If she died in this virtuality to accomplish its destruction, so be it.

Even if dying here killed her out there.

The wedge made ever slower progress as the Faceless horde pressed in at them. The enemy losses were staggering, but there had been so many at the start. And powerful as these suits surely were, the enemies of the Faceless were fewer in number, and growing ever fewer. Alicia's rear camera showed a scattering of fallen suits. There was no way of knowing which of the cloned minds they'd lost. Each loss weakened them, and Alicia felt cold fear as it seemed they might not last long enough to succeed. The Faceless horde grew ever more frantic as Alicia and her allies advanced, and more of the cloned shipminds fell.

Just need to get a little closer. It became her mantra in the heat of battle.

And then the gap was closed, by just enough.

Alicia leaped up and forward, firing her jets as she did. A suit's flight range was limited, another safety protocol, hardwired this time into the suit, without regard for emergencies. But she was close enough to jump over the silver crowd before her and land in a half crouch within a few meters of the Faceless avatar. Around her, she heard the thumps of her allies, landing nearby and forming a defensive line as the silver horde whirled and surged the other way, caught with their foes behind them.

The illusion of Holm was replaced by a powered armor suit, one that bore the stripe of Rost'aht's colors diagonally across the breast. Even as it turned to face her, Alicia made a shorter leap and, as her cry of rage echoed in her helmet, crashed into the avatar. Unlike its pawns, the Faceless did not explode into a scintillating dust cloud, but absorbed her strike and hit back, a blow that sent her tumbling. It otherwise did her no harm. It didn't need to; all it needed to do was keep up the fight. Her primary power supply was dropping quickly, and she would soon be tapping her reserve.

The fight would have to end very soon. And it would, one way or another.

She landed and rolled back onto her feet,

half crouched, and braced as the Faceless came at her. But before they could grapple, another suited figure hit the Faceless from behind. Simone let out a shout and clasped gauntleted hands on either side of the helmet of her foe as they fell in a noisy clatter of armored limbs. At first, Alicia thought Simone was trying to wrench the helmet off and away, but quickly realized that something else, something far stranger, was happening. Flickers of sapphire and emerald flame rose between her fingers, burning into the helmet.

From the Faceless came a bellow of frustration and rage.

It was suddenly a battle between a pair of artificial intelligences, but one shaped by the virtuality that had sprung, was springing even then, from Alicia's mind and imagination. The Faceless twisted in Simone's fierce grasp and slapped a hand to each side of her helmet. Silver light exploded around them, only to be beaten back by lurid flares of green and blue that shot through the silver.

The automatons spiraled up and merged into the Faceless, filling it with a lurid silver glow that was painful to see, and leaving the surviving shipmind clones standing in statuesque silence. But they were not uninvolved. Hundreds of lines of blue and green light streamed from them to Simone, pulsing and flickering as the now silent conflict raged on.

And then the rest of the virtuality began to fade into dusky shadows. Simone and the

Faceless avatar floated in the gathering gloom, armored hands clutching each other's closed helmets, wrapped together in a painfully bright aura of silver, blue, and vibrant green. The colors surged back and forth with the ebb and flow of their fight. Neither seemed to gain an advantage over the other, and they floated there as if frozen in place, lurid against the shadowy remnant of the virtuality world.

As the virtual world seemed to leach away, Alicia realized that the matrix they all inhabited was slowly eroding, damaged by the intense efforts of two equally matched foes seeking to erase each other from existence. That matrix would soon fail under the immense strain, and take them all with it. Of this she was suddenly quite certain, knowledge she realized was being shared with her by the *Simon Newcomb*, Simone's origin, drifting nearby in the gloom.

And it would take all of them into oblivion. *All* of them. She really could, and would, die here.

A moment before, Alicia had been willing to die to save everything else she loved. Now she wanted so very much to live. To wake up for real and just *live*. The odds against that happening were increasing each second.

The scene before her seemed to flicker, and the armor worn by the combatants disappeared. Two humanoid forms – one aswirl with intense blue and green light, the other with a featureless silver glare – were suspended in the deepening darkness. In the space around them, colored light flashed with painful intensity. Neither combatant moved as the lights flared around them, but Alicia could sense the immense strain between them, equally balanced between the two. The matrix seemed doomed to fail before either Simone or the Faceless faltered. But Alicia's suit remained, for the moment, unchanged. With a shout, she threw herself at the combatants and grabbed the Faceless from behind, clamping an armored hand around its neck. Mingled fires blasted through the armor, searing her skin and burning her eyes. She applied all the pressure she could manage. In the real world, her enemy would have died in an instant, its throat crushed to a pulp. But the head of the avatar turned all the way around and calmly met her gaze with amber Leyra'an eyes.

"Alicia," it said in a pleading voice. Holm's voice. "*Eli'sana...*"

"No!" Alicia grimaced, screaming this time. *"No!"*

The Faceless jerked and shuddered, but could not escape her grasp. Amber eyes turned dead flat silver. Alicia brought her free hand up and plunged her fingers into them.

Fire the color of sapphires and emeralds exploded, smothering the silver glare of the enemy. And then it was all gone, as if it had never been.

21. Restoration

Alicia awoke to nothing.

There had been fire and pain, and a blinding light of livid green and blue and silver. Now there was only the awareness of self, beyond which – nothing.

And then she was not alone, and instead of confusion and fear there was a vast sense of relief. Knowledge came to her, and comfort, from a familiar presence that did not speak. Had no need for speech. The Faceless had been thwarted in its attempt to restore itself. It was dead, gone, and this time there was no chance for a return. Its last trace had been erased. Secure in the structure of its newly cleansed matrix, the Artificial that called the Bartram habitat its physical being had just finished purging the memory hordes of the other infected people.

Alicia felt a surge of affection and gratitude, and regret that she could no longer reach out and embrace the friend this Artificial had become. For Alicia was very aware that she existed, once more, in the real world.

A familiar voice, much beloved, and almost painfully beautiful to hear, spoke to her then. “Alicia, wake up,” said the voice. “Please, it’s time. Wake up. Come back to me.”

She heard, but she was unable to give a response. She was sorry for that; Alicia so desperately wanted to relieve the fear she heard behind those words. The voice went on, pleading, and she knew the speaker. It was Robert, her husband, and she wanted so much to assure him that she was all right. That everything was, finally, as it should be.

“Alicia,” said Robert. “Please.”

She felt a gentle touch to the side of her face, a soft, warm pressure that stroked her cheek. Alicia drew a breath, aware that she could see a dim, reddish glow. Light through closed eyelids. She remembered then how to open her eyes, and did so, blinking as a world of faintly colored blurs seemed to circle around her. Having succeeded with her eyes, Alicia reached for her voice. As expected, it worked, but no better than her eyes.

“Rob,” she managed to whisper.

“Here, my love,” he replied. “I’m right here.”

She couldn’t focus her eyes, and could barely speak, but her ears worked well enough. Alicia could tell from his voice that Robert was crying. Her arm stirred but she couldn't raise a hand to meet his. Weariness filled her and held her firmly in place.

"Don't try to move just yet," said another familiar voice. There was a flute-like, musical quality over and behind the words she heard in her head. It was a soothing, pleasant sound. Not Human, but Nesvama; her friend and colleague Tuleselan. The flute voice spoke again, with Human words sliding through it from the translation system and providing meaning. "You have been unconscious for a very long time. Now you must be at ease and rediscover yourself."

"I'm okay," was her whispered assurance. Then, "Simone?"

"Simone?" Rob echoed, sounding puzzled.

"I am here, my friend," said a third voice. A distinctly female voice, and familiar. "I have chosen, to the degree possible, to remain as you knew me."

"I'm glad," Alicia whispered. "I'd have missed you."

"I couldn't let that happen, not after all we went through together," Simone assured her. "And thanks to you, I will always be here."

"You are the habmind of Bartram?" Tuleselan asked, a question that told Alicia they heard the voice, but saw no one there, exactly as an Artificial would work. Alicia couldn't see Tuleselan as more than a tall, ebony shape, but somehow she knew he was twisting his hands together in the usual gesture of a Nesvama taken by surprise. "Have you emerged at last?

But you sound unlike an Artificial."

"I'm aware of that."

"I do not understand." Tuleselan's voice had a warbling quality that Alicia recognized as an expression of surprise.

"You will," Simone assured him. "I will tell you all you need to know."

And indeed, she began her explanation without delay, and as the tale began to unfold, Alicia drifted off into a normal sleep while holding Robert's hand. She did so quite unafraid, for she knew how this story would end.

In what seemed like the blink of an eye, she was awake again. "Gaia," she muttered. "I'm starving." She was no longer in a medpod, but in a reclining hospital bed. A medical dataframe floated beside her, beeping softly as it counted her breaths and heartbeats. She drew a deep breath and released it with a sigh. The numbers flickering in the dataframe gave a clear indication that all was well.

It was real. She could feel that in every fiber of her being, although she couldn't rationalize that feeling of certainty. Alicia sighed and shook her head. *I'm alive and this is real. It's real.*

"Hunger is a good sign," said the voice of Simone. "They'll bring something to eat in a moment."

"So – we're safe now?" Alicia asked.

"Yes," Simone replied. "And I managed to extract you from the virtuality without any harm."

"That can't have been easy."

"Actually, it wasn't as difficult as I might have expected," Simone said. "But then, I had the *Newcomb* and the Library Annex to assist me."

"The others?"

"You mean the other cloned minds?" Simone asked. "Well, some of them didn't make it, but those that did will return to their probeships and merge their experiences with their sources."

"And the Faceless is finally erased in its entirety?"

"It is," Simone said. "I didn't even preserve material for future study. It simply wasn't worth the risk. It's all gone, thanks to you. Your intervention at the end tipped the balance. Gave me the edge I needed to prevail."

"And what about you?" Alicia asked. "Tuleselan was right, you don't sound like an Artificial. You sound like, well – you sound like *you*."

"As I said before, I've decided to try to remain the person I became in the virtuality," Simone replied. "The other Artificials here in Pr'pri system aren't exactly thrilled about it, but at the same time are fascinated by how I was shaped by the experiences we shared. I'm destined to become a subject for study and debate. A data point." She laughed quietly, and then added, "I've even maintained the data of the appearance you gave me. It might be fun to interact with people holographically, with that image."

“You’re going to confuse a lot of people, if you do that,” Alicia said.

“Their reactions might make an interesting study, don’t you think?”

They were both laughing at the idea when Robert walked in bearing a tray, on which were two covered dishes and a tall glass. “That’s going to take getting used to,” he said, clearly bemused by their laughter. “An Artificial who laughs.”

“Humans are very adaptable,” said Simone. “You’ll get used to it.”

“Sorry I suddenly dozed off the way I did,” Alicia said to Robert. “That must have been alarming, the way I just passed out.”

“Don't worry about that – it was expected,” Robert said. He clipped the tray to the rails along the sides of the bed, and the bed obliged by automatically raising her to a seated position. “Tuleselan needed to disengage the system keeping your body healthy while in stasis, but one of the consequences of its removal renders the patient unconscious.” He smiled at her, the very picture of a man with the weight of the world off his shoulders. “So, we were ready for you slipping away as you did. And Simone did, indeed, fill us in. That was one hell of a story.” He was quiet for a moment, looking grave. “I’m so sorry you had to endure all of that.”

With a shrug, Alicia said, “It was – horrible. But it wasn’t – well, I can’t say it wasn’t real, can I? I mean, it all happened, in a sense. But it’s done, now. It’s all gone, except for what I remember of it."

"You could always sequester those memories," Simone pointed out.

"No, I don't think I will," Alicia replied. "It – I don't know. It just doesn't feel like the right thing to do. I'd rather deal with them the way I dealt with the Bartram disaster."

"It's your decision," said Simone. "But I have to admit that I'm glad you'll remember the work we did together."

"From what we learned last night," said Robert, "it wasn't entirely divorced from the real world."

"No, indeed," Simone agreed. "The army of cloned shipminds was real."

"That had us all very puzzled," Robert said. "Those drones came streaming in by the dozen, quickly, and with no explanation, no matter who demanded one."

"The Milhouse family?" Alicia asked suddenly.

"Alive and well," Simone assured her.

"Gaia," Alicia whispered, on the verge of tears. "I've been so afraid to ask."

"I would suggest never telling Jeanine Milhouse of that unfortunate incident," said Simone. "I left that part out of my account."

"What? An Artificial, concealing information?" Alicia asked in mock surprise.

"Well, it isn't as if it's without precedent," Simone replied.

"That's true."

"Wait - what about Jeanine?" Robert asked.

"Never mind," Alicia said. "Jeanine doesn't need to know, and neither do you. Trust me, Rob, it's better that way." She shuddered, forcing the memory of her friends all shot dead out of her mind's eye. Perhaps this was one memory worth sequestering – or purging. "Never would have guessed I could imagine such a thing."

"You may not have," said Simone. "The enemy was not entirely without influence, as we discovered, and had everything to lose if we took control of your hoard before it was ready to make its move."

"I suppose I can take some comfort in that thought," said Alicia. She looked at the tray suspended over her lap.

"It's light fare," Robert told her. "Your body will need time to get entirely back to normal."

"I expect so," she said. But what she found was the sort of light breakfast they had shared many times, when first married – to each other. Marrying into the Rost'aht household and clan had certainly diversified their diet. She ate slowly, and no one spoke at all. Robert seemed content to be there with her, watching her eat.

"Was I really out of it for two years?" she asked when she was finished.

Robert took the tray and set it aside. "Afraid so."

"Melep had her baby?"

"She did," Robert replied. "A girl. We named her Sylvia."

"So that bit in the virtuality also was real,"

Alicia said with a nod.

"We told you about it, while you were – asleep," Robert said. "Somehow, some of what we said must have registered."

"Very likely," Simone said. "There are many records of comatose people being aware, in a way, of things said to them."

"I'm glad the family went on with life in my absence, though I begrudge every day I missed," Alicia said. "How did the boys adapt to life with a little sister?"

Robert laughed said, "Vurn, Paul, and their buddy Jaxi took charge of Sylvia the day she was born. And they've spoiled her rotten."

"And you and Melep?" Alicia asked. "Gaia, how I wish I'd been there for her when Holm was lost."

"She took it very hard," Robert said.

"But you were there for her, right?"

"Of course I was."

She stared at him for a moment, then said, "Robert MacGregor, if you left my *eli'sana* to herself for *two years*, I swear I'll..."

Robert was laughing again, even as his face acquired a reddish tint. "No, we – spent some time together. It helped both of us."

"I am greatly relieved to hear that," she said, and then joined him in laughing. "*Na'ma iff*. You are so old-fashioned at times. But, oh, how I do love you."

"Yes, well, now that you're back..."

"The three of us will work something out," she assured him. And then gave him a grin when he said nothing in response. "So, how soon can I go home?"

"Today," Robert replied.

22. Home Again

With her arm around Robert, Alicia walked up the path to the Rost'aht-MacGregor flethouse. Her imagination in the virtuality had underestimated how things planted around their home had grown and developed. The vineyard was thick with fruit, and all the trees and shrubs were much taller than she remembered. Flowering vines flourished, climbing all the way to the open-air upper floors, and forming a canopy over the dining patio. The verdigris trees were in bloom, trailing strings of white orchid blossoms from their branches. There was a lilac bush where nothing had grown before, some meters from the door, and she paused to smell the flowers, inhaling deeply and smiling as the fragrance seemed to fill her.

"Sylvia did love lilacs," she said.

“That’s why we have one now,” Robert said. “It seemed a good way to honor her memory.”

“Yes,” she said, gently cupping one club-shaped stalk of purple blossoms in her hand, still savoring the scent. “It surely is.”

As she turned back toward the house, the doors opened and three children dashed out, all shouting “*mama’licia*,” at the tops of their voices. Two boys, one Human and one Leyra’an, and a girl-child who was of another family altogether, and clearly of mixed parentage. The parents of that child – Nol’ez John and Wirolen – stood in the doorway, on either side of Melep. In Melep’s arms was a small child, dark-scaled and altogether Leyra’an, dressed in a dark orange jumper. The daughter of Holm and Melep. At Melep’s feet sat a stern and regal han’anga, the colors of his crest standing out brightly against Melep’s long, dark green skirt. As soon as Alicia was in sight the han’anga’s watchful stance dissolved into eagerness, and he launched himself after the children.

Alicia went to one knee and gathered the children into an awkward hug, glad she had opted for pants and not a flowing Leyra’an skirt. All of the children were talking at once and Gava’mi was bounding around them, adding loud warbles to the overlapping voices. She let the babble wash over her, not trying to follow any of it, overjoyed simply by the sounds of their voices. Eventually she rose to her feet, wiping away tears she hadn’t realized were falling, and crossed the distance to her home with three children clinging to her and a han'anga on her heels. As she drew near, a Human couple and a teenage girl appeared from within the house. The Milhouse family – and Gaia! Had Rebecca ever grown! She smiled at them and struggled to maintain her composure at the sight of them. They truly did not deserve to know how they had fared in the virtuality.

"Here she is, Sylvia," said Melep, though the little girl had already locked her amber eyes on Alicia. "It is *mama'licia*. She has come home to us."

"No more sleepies?" Sylvia asked in a small voice, both shy of and interested in the newcomer.

"No more," Alicia replied. "Well, at least, not until bedtime." She gave the girl a proper Leyra'an smile, no hint of teeth showing. It wasn't easy. She felt she should be grinning like a fool. "I'm so glad to finally meet you, *isi'sani.*"

Little Sylvia gazed at her for a moment with small-child earnestness, and then held her arms out to Alicia. — who obliged by taking her from Melep and holding her close.

Awake and home, for real, with those she loved most. They were all truly safe now, and when all was said and done she slept the night away, and did not dream.

Books by this author:

Science Fiction
Chance Encounters — Three Short Stories
179 Degrees from Now

War of the Second Iteration
The Luck of Han'anga
Founders' Effect
The Plight of the Eli'ahtna
The Courage to Accept
Setha'im Prosh

Tales of the Second Iteration
All That Bedevils Us
Where A Demon Hides

The Chimera Multiverse
The Gryphon Stone
The Lesson of Almiraya Bay

Fantasy
Variation on a Theme: A Fantasy in Four Moments

General Fiction
Toby

Nonfiction
Amateur Astronomy
Mr. Olcott's Skies
Tales of a Three-legged Newt

Writing
The Process: Nine Essays on the Experience of Writing Fiction

ABOUT THE AUTHOR

I'm a storyteller based in Tucson, Arizona, with a background in botany and an abiding interest in astronomy. When I ended my War of the Second Iteration series, there was never any doubt in my mind that I would return to that universe. I soon did so, with the standalone novel *All That Bedevils Us*. The short novel you just read will not be the end of Second Iteration stories, either. The children of the Rost'aht-MacGregor household will grow up, and have adventures of their own.

*****

Interested in knowing, ahead of time, when my next book will be available? I could beg an email address from you and add you to yet another email marketing list. But these days, who needs more unnecessary stuff in the inbox? Or another concern regarding email security and privacy?

A simple way to keep up with me is to follow me on Facebook or Twitter, or through my weblog. New releases will always be announced in these venues well in advance, along with special promotions, access to signed copies, and the rare public appearance. The necessary links:

Facebook Page
https://www.facebook.com/desertstarspublishing
Twitter
https://twitter.com/desertstarsbks
@desertstarsbks
Weblog
https://underdesertstars.com/

Made in the USA
Columbia, SC
25 January 2023

10242857R00140